# The Magic Locker

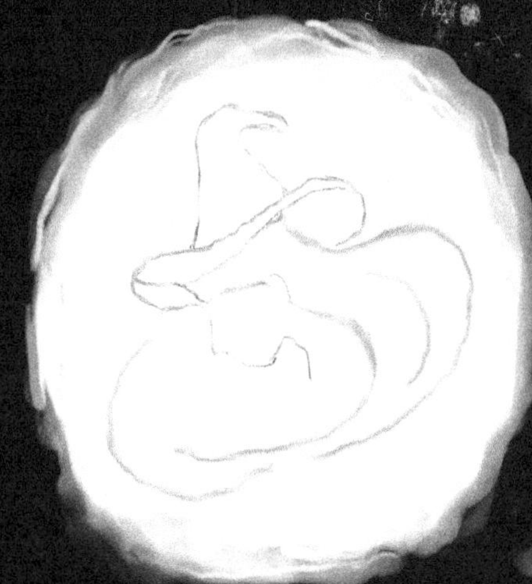

# THE WITCH'S CURSE

WORDS AND ILLUSTRATIONS BY

# ELARA DUNN

Cover by Devma Zed

# Contents

This book is dedicated to all those who suffer at the hands of another. May you discover the magic that lives inside you.

Embrace your power,

Elara XOXO

# Prologue

Children's stories tell of the battle between good and evil. The hero overcomes various obstacles to defeat the villain, and they all live happily ever after.

This is not a tale for children.

You will soon discover that the lines between good and evil are blurred; that when a door opens, another side is revealed.

Prepare yourself, for the Magic Locker is about to be opened.

# Chapter 1

# Eleanor McNeil

Ellie McNeil walked down the sidewalk towards her very first day of high school. Despite enduring years of bullying, Ellie was still hopeful things would turn around for her.

*"This is my year!"* she thought, *"High school will be so much better! The kids will be so much more mature. No more bullying!"*

She couldn't help but feel relieved that Tiffany-Ann Trombley had moved away over the summer. Tiffany-Ann had made Ellie's life a living hell since kindergarten. Tiffany-Ann had pushed Ellie off the slide on the first day, and the humiliation hadn't stopped since. Even the name Tiffany-Ann Trombley made Ellie shudder with fear. That was the problem with small towns. Once you had a target on your back, you could never shake it. As soon as Tiffany-Ann started torturing Ellie, the other kids followed suit. It was self-preservation.

Still, Ellie liked the small-town freedom of being able to walk everywhere. Her parents had given her more independence that summer, with the stipulation that she check in from time to time. Ellie's friendship with Angela Anders had grown into full BFF status with that new-found independence. Angela had been an acquaintance, a fellow student with a target on her back as well. Ellie ran into Angela while shopping at the mall with her mother at the beginning of the summer. They clicked right away. Their shared experience of being bullied helped Ellie feel much less alone. Their text conversations and trips to the movies made it the best summer Ellie ever had. Yes, she would focus on seeing Angela at school and tune everyone else out.

Ellie stiffened her lips as she approached the school entrance, in an attempt to look more formidable. The taunts started as soon as she walked through the front doors.

*"Nice bag McNeil. Whose corpse did you get that from?"*

*"Oh my god...did you see her shoes?"*

*"Keep walking, Ellie, keep walking..."* she told herself, keeping her head held high.

*"Hey Ellie, nice glasses, loser!"*

Ellie spun around so fast that her ponytail smacked her in the face.

"All the better to see you with!" she shouted.

Sigh. *"Seriously? Red Riding Hood?"* she thought to herself. *"That's so second grade. I will have to write down some better comebacks later."*

Ellie couldn't help but wonder when the other kids got so big as she made her way to her locker. She kept an eye out for Angela but didn't see her. She searched for her locker, number G09. She reached it and pulled out the slip of paper with the combination written on it.

*"Hey, Ellie can't remember her locker combination! What an idiot!"*

This was easier to tune out. Nothing turned that frown upside-down like a new purple locker rug. Ellie proceeded to decorate the locker with mobiles of various planets, glow-in-the-dark stars, and posters of her favorite band, the incomparably dark and moody My Sister Cellophane. She saved the purple rug, the pièce de résistance, for last. As she carefully smoothed the rug across the bottom of the locker, she saw a quick flash of light in the locker's back corner, like a candle being lit. She turned around to see what the locker was reflecting, but there was nothing. She stared at the back of the locker for a moment.

The bell rang, and Ellie realized she was about to be late for her very first class on her very first day at Cecilia Payne High School. That is no way to make a first impression. She ran for it and got through the door to the math room just in time. Sweaty, panting, and disheveled, but on time.

She made her way to the first available seat, trying to act like she hadn't just run across the entire length of the school.

*"Wow, this high school is a lot bigger than our middle school,"* she reflected as she opened her laptop, ready to go.

A whisper came from behind her: *"Your backpack smells like an old lady."*

Nope, Ellie would not be provoked again. She glanced over at the other students hoping to see Angela, but there was no sign of her. Maybe next class. Why didn't they compare schedules last week?

*"I love your skirt. Purple used to be my favorite color, too. Like, in third grade,"* muttered the voice from behind her.

The teacher, Mrs. Canter, turned from the whiteboard, glowering in Ellie's general direction. "I will not have any talking in my class."

Ellie turned beet red as some of her classmates snickered, but she kept her composure.

*"Nice patches. Covering the stains from the previous owner?"*

Focus, Ellie.

"Quiet!" warned the teacher while writing the first equation.

*"You know that the guys in My Sister Cellophane are gay, right?"*

Dang it.

Ellie swung around and shouted, "And what's wrong with...." But trailed off as she came face-to-face with a girl she did not know...a terrifyingly tall, muscular, and beautiful girl. A girl who was so intimidating it stopped Ellie's words from coming out of her mouth. A girl who was sure to become a new and improved sort of bully.

"Eleanor McNeil, go straight to the principal's office!" Ellie had forgotten herself for a moment, but the teacher's words snapped her back to her present circumstances. Ellie gathered up her old lady backpack, straightened her third grade purple skirt, pushed up her glasses, and mustered all the dignity she had left as she headed to the principal's office.

"McNeil, McNeil. Eleanor McNeil." Ok, well, Principal Martinez proved he knew her name. "Eleanor, high school can be a big adjustment. Sometimes you have to go out and be ready for the pass."

*"Wait. Is that football? Is he using sports analogies?"* thought Ellie.

"Some kids feel pressure to be disruptive. Don't let the other kids pressure you into dropping that ball. Being cool means being a team player."

*"Yeah, this is totally football."* Ellie imagined her awkward self in full football gear.

"I see your grades from last year are excellent. I'll let you off with a warning. But no more outbursts. I suggest you check in with Dr. Sophia, the school counselor. She can help you stay on track towards the goalpost."

"Ok, I'll be sure to do that!" she answered while thinking, *"No, I won't."* "Thank you, Principal Martinez!"

As Ellie left the principal's office, she thought, *"Welp, it can't get any worse!"*

• • • ●•● • • •

And this, precisely, is our teachings from children's books. Keep your chin up, and all will be well. Ellie gets married and has lots of kids who never shit, make a mess, or steal the car. But this is not a children's book, and Ellie will learn better than to think positively.

# Chapter 2

# A Flash of Fury

Ellie woke up the next morning refreshed and ready. She would not let the events of the previous day dampen her mood. After all, she's bound to run into Angela today. Ellie recalled when she and Angela had met at the beach that summer. It was the first time Ellie had been there since she was a little girl. Calling it a beach might be unfair; it was a tiny, man-made lake with a tiny, man-made patch of sand, and a tiny playground, which one could only assume was also man-made. Ellie often went there as a child and played happily by herself. One day, older boys were throwing firecrackers against the wall of the concession stand, which never seemed to be open. Ellie was building a magnificent sand castle when a firecracker landed right next to her. She was never certain whether it was intentional or not. The explosion did not hurt Ellie, but the noise scared her. She ran home crying, never to return until that day Angela suggested they meet there.

Ellie had also been looking forward to concert band starting. Concert band only rehearsed three days out of the week, with study hall on the other two. The one skill Ellie had was playing trombone. It's not fair to say her parents forced her to learn it, but she was strongly encouraged to give it a go. She ended up being good at it. Besides, it was one of her few means of social interaction. Band geeks stick together.

Ellie attempted to tame her curly hair. No matter what she did, it always ended up making it look worse. She stared in the mirror, trying not to be disappointed at the reflection staring back at her. With a heavy sigh, she put her hair up into a ponytail, trying to pin back the defiant strands that somehow never made it into the tie. She managed to smile at her reflection before heading downstairs for a quick breakfast with her parents. She headed to school, grasping onto that good-mood feeling she woke up with while trying to ignore the general insults being slung her way.

After enduring taunts and various small items being thrown at her from the terrifying girl during math class, Ellie headed to the science room. Science had always been difficult for Ellie, but as luck would have it, freshman year started with basic astronomy. Ellie had loved learning about outer space for as long as she could remember. Her parents had a giant book about the solar system full of fun facts and photos. She imagined how much better life would be on other planets. When she learned no evidence of life had been discovered yet, it only slightly dampened her enthusiasm. Things just had to be better somewhere.

"Eleanor McNeil, can you tell me the names of the planets?" asked Mr. Joshi. Why, yes, she could.

"Mercury, Venus, Earth, Mars, Jupiter, Saturn, Uranus," several kids snickered at this. So much for high school being more mature. Ellie continued, "and Neptune. I will include Pluto even though it's been demoted."

*"What a dork."*

Ellie cared not. She had always been pro-Pluto.

"Excellent, Ms. McNeil," praised Mr. Joshi.

Okay, so the day was going well after all. Ellie grabbed her old-lady backpack with renewed confidence and headed toward her locker. She pulled out the piece of paper with the combination written on it.

*"Oh my god, you don't have that memorized yet?"*

*"Get a clue, McNeil!"*

*"What a loser!"*

Ellie struggled to focus on the combination. The more she tried, the less she could concentrate.

*"Have you seen her bag? Those patches are hideous!"*

*"When was the last time you showered, Smelly Ellie?"*

Ellie choked back tears. She wouldn't let them get to her. *"Just open the locker, get what you need, and get to class,"* she told herself.

*"Do us all a favor and wear a bag over your head."*

*"Is she crying? Is Ellie actually crying?"*

The voices started to amplify in Ellie's head as the taunts swarmed around her. Tears began to fall down her cheeks. Suddenly, her locker popped open. She was sure she hadn't finished the combination yet. She grabbed her English book and hurried to class, composing herself along the way. Where was Angela? She really needed her. Ellie resolved to text Angela that night if she did not see her today. It would be all right once she could talk to her friend. Angela would understand.

· · · ● · ● · ● · · ·

By band time, Ellie had brushed off the event at her locker. She grabbed her trombone from the back storage room and found her seat. She was relieved to be sitting next to Paul Whitmore. Ellie wasn't exactly friends with Paul. They sat next to each other in the middle school band, sometimes sharing a laugh. They nodded to each other as she sat. She looked around the band room nervously, noticing all the unfamiliar older students.

*"Nice backpack,"* mused a voice behind her. Oh, come on, really? Ellie whipped around to face her assailant.

"My Sister Cellophane has some talent, but I prefer harder stuff, like War Tank" continued the girl behind her, sporting a half-cocked smile.

"Um, thanks," replied Ellie hesitantly, sensing a trap. The girl had long blue hair shaved on one side and angled down to a point covering half of her face. Ellie pointed to a red anarchy symbol on the girl's left arm. "Is that a tattoo?"

"Nah. My parents won't let me get one. I'm using marker until I'm old enough to get a real one."

"Oh, um, cool," replied Ellie, still hesitant.

"Trombone. Bold choice for a chick. I prefer my drum set, but Mr. Schwartz has no vision and put me on timpani instead."

"Yeah, my parents made me play trombone, but I really wanted to play bass." Ellie was growing more confident now.

"Spectacular! The bass guitar is the heart of any band!"

Ellie actually meant stand-up bass but was too embarrassed to correct her enthusiastic new friend.

"Nicole Faisal, I see you haven't outgrown your penchant for talking during class over the summer." The booming voice caused Ellie to bolt straight up in her seat. She turned to see the band director, Mr. Schwartz, standing at the conductor's stand with a kind but impatient grin. "Now, if you're finished with what was undoubtedly a fascinating conversation, I would like to begin class."

"Just recruiting more members to the dark side, Mr. Schwartz." Nicole playfully retorted with a wink to Ellie, "Please feel free to start now."

Ellie was aghast. She had never met anyone like Nicole Faisal before. So bold, so cool...so free. Ellie was deep in thought about her new acquaintance as she left the band room. When she reached her locker, she was surprised to see that Angela Anders was walking towards her. Finally! A wave of relief washed over her. Ellie didn't know what to start with...a hug, a witty phrase, unloading about her terrifying new assailant? She smiled to greet Angela. Angela stopped in her tracks, looked around the crowded hallway with a panicked look upon her face, and yelled, "Oh my god, Ellie. You are so ugly!"

Ellie's world came crashing down. She quickly opened her locker to hide her face. Everyone was laughing, especially the terrifying girl and her crew. Why would Angela say that? What happened to their friendship? The fun they had over the summer? Ellie imagined a flash of light coming from within the locker to match her flash of fury.

Except she didn't imagine it.

What happened next was all a blur. Ellie spun around, and her backpack met with Angela's face. Shouting and fighting broke out in the hallway. Ellie saw Principal Martinez heading towards her and Angela. Bracing for the worst, Ellie started to explain herself. Principal Martinez held up his hand to stop her.

"Miss, I want you to report to my office immediately." Ellie was startled to see Mr. Martinez pointing to Angela instead of her.

"What? *She* hit *me*!!!" screamed an astounded Angela.

"No arguments. I'll meet you in my office." Angela stomped towards the principal's office. Mr. Martinez gave Ellie a wink and headed off after Angela, disappearing into the crowd.

Ellie turned back to her locker. There was no denying the glow inside of it now. No one else seemed to notice. Ellie leaned into the locker. She heard an unsettling voice, weak and wavering, but the words were clear.

"Embrace your power."

# Chapter 3

# Angela and the Horrible Thing

Ellie barely slept that night. There was too much rattling around in her brain. Why did Angela say that thing, that horrible thing? Ellie couldn't bear to even think about the actual words. The betrayal wounded her so deeply, so profoundly, that she could feel a fire burn in the pit of her stomach. And the conversations they had! Ellie confided everything to Angela! Would Angela tell everyone about Ellie's worries? Her secret crushes? Her insecurities? What would Ellie do? What *could* she do?

But the locker, the locker was more troublesome. Lockers do not emit light, and they certainly don't speak to you. Surely Ellie had imagined it all. It was too much stress. Yes, that must be it. Ellie wouldn't hurt the proverbial fly, nonetheless a person. The shock of Angela and the horrible thing caused her to snap. She thought maybe she should check in with Dr. Sophia after all.

On top of that, Ellie realized she would have to face the terrifying new girl in math class again. She wasn't sure how much more she could take. Maybe she could pretend to be sick. No, her mother would see right through it; she always did. Ellie put on her glasses, got out of bed, and got dressed for school. She tucked her curls into her signature ponytail and took a long look at herself in the mirror. She knew it was time to face the day. Her reflection didn't seem so sure.

Ellie checked in with the office to make an appointment with the counselor when she arrived at school. She chose the time slot directly after math in case she had more problems with the terrifying girl. Ellie held her breath as she approached her locker. There was no avoiding it. She stared at the locker, afraid to open it.

"That was a brave thing you did yesterday," said a voice, startling Ellie. She turned to face the speaker. "I never had the nerve to hit anyone back," he continued. The boy was tall and lanky, wearing a suit jacket that was much too big for him with a big silk flower on the lapel paired with skinny black jeans. His blond hair tousled over his too-pale face. He stared at Ellie intently, like he wanted to say something else. The look was unnervingly dark. Finally, he broke his gaze. He cheerfully waved with a ridiculous flourish as he walked away, bouncing on his heels, shouting, "Okay, bye!"

*"I have no time for that kind of weird right now,"* thought Ellie. *"Time to open this totally normal locker and prove my insanity."*

The locker popped open before she even touched it. A tiny ball of light zipped around the back of it. She turned to see if anyone else noticed. Everyone went about their business. She did notice there were fewer jeers in her general direction than usual. No one else seemed to notice the magical locker.

"Embrace your power," the same eerie voice whispered to her, stronger than yesterday but still wavering.

Ellie slammed the locker shut and ran to math class in a panic. She arrived once again sweaty, panting, and disheveled, but on time. Sure enough, the terrifying girl smirked menacingly at Ellie as she took her seat.

"Open your books to page ten, please," Mrs. Canter said sternly, "Eleanor McNeil, can you tell me what x equals in the first problem?"

Why, no, she couldn't.

"Uh... four?"

Mrs. Canter peered at Ellie momentarily, then asked, "Olivia Hurley, can you tell me what x equals in the first problem?"

"I believe it is two, Mrs. Canter," answered the terrifying girl in an overly-sugary voice. Of course.

"Correct, Ms. Hurley," stated Mrs. Canter, then turned to the whiteboard. Ellie sunk into her seat.

*"Good job, Smelly Ellie,"* teased the voice of the terrifying Olivia Hurley from behind her. The fire in Ellie's stomach started to burn again. Yes, this one is sure to be worse than Tiffany-Ann Trombley.

*"You're such a dumbass."*

Ellie concentrated hard to follow Mrs. Canter's lecture. Oliva Hurley was relentless.

*"And you're so ugly!"*

So ugly. The horrible thing Angela said. The fire in Ellie's stomach was bursting. She started to feel dizzy. Everything started to blur....

Ellie snapped back into focus to the sound of a large crash behind her. She spun around to see that a bookshelf had fallen over onto the floor next to Olivia. Olivia looked shaken but unharmed. Mrs. Canter was heading down the aisle to investigate.

"Are you all right, Ms. Hurley?" Olivia nodded her head. Mrs. Canter resumed class. Ellie glanced over her shoulder to see Olivia glaring at her.

· · · ● · ● · ● · · ·

On her way to Dr. Sophia's office, Ellie frantically wondered if she had knocked over the bookcase somehow. She didn't remember anything except feeling a flash of anger. Did she black out? The bookcase seemed too big for Ellie to have moved it on her own. Surely someone would have seen her do it? Mrs. Canter didn't seem to suspect her at all.

Ellie stood at Dr. Sophia's door. Maybe she should ditch the appointment. After all, she couldn't tell Dr. Sophia the truth. No, she would just say she forgot about the session.

The door opened as Ellie turned to leave. A tall, dark-haired woman wearing a well-tailored black pantsuit with a white ruffled shirt peeking out underneath stood in the doorway. Ellie thought the woman looked more like an international spy than a school counselor. She had an air of darkness and intrigue about her.

"Eleanor McNeill?" the woman asked. "I'm Dr. Sophia."

They proceeded through a small waiting room on their way to Dr. Sophia's office. Ellie entered the office and was half-relieved and half-disappointed that there was no couch to lie on while divulging her deepest, darkest secrets. She sat in a chair across from the counselor's desk, a much less dramatic seating option.

"What brings you in today, Eleanor?" Dr. Sophia asked kindly.

*"Well, I have a glowing magic locker that speaks to me, and I may be hurting people, but I don't know if I'm doing it because I'm blacking out,"* thought Ellie. Best wait until the second session for that.

"Um, Principal Martinez suggested I come," muttered Ellie uncertainly, "Oh, and I go by Ellie." Ellie wasn't at all sure why she added in that last part. All of her teachers called her Eleanor.

"Okay, Ellie, why were you in Principal Martinez's office?"

Ellie told Dr. Sophia about the incident with Olivia Hurley that landed her in the principal's office. In fact, she told her much more of it than she had intended. There was something about Dr. Sophia that made Ellie feel she could trust her, that she would understand. Of course, Ellie made no mention of the locker. Dr. Sophia listened and nodded, sometimes asking for clarification but otherwise allowing Ellie to talk.

"Do you have many friends at school?"

Before she could stop herself, Ellie started retelling the story of Angela Anders. Once again, she omitted the glowing locker, blacking out (did she black out?), and the backpack incident, but expressed her devastation and frustration over the betrayal. She confessed her relief that Tiffany-Ann Trombley had moved away, but was scared that she would move back someday. She divulged a particularly humiliating incident where Tiffany-Ann had chased Ellie around the gym track in middle school. Everyone had cheered Tiffany-Ann on. The gym teacher didn't intervene until after Tiffany-Ann had knocked Ellie to the ground and started kicking her. When she finished her story, Dr. Sophia stopped typing and looked hard at Ellie. It was a look that conveyed sympathy, sadness, and warmth all at the same time somehow. Ellie felt as if Dr. Sophia was staring into her very soul. It should have been unnerving, but Ellie felt a great comfort from it.

Dr. Sophia broke her gaze. "Thank you for confiding in me, Ellie. That must have been very difficult for you. Have you ever tried deep breathing exercises?" Ellie had not. They spent the rest of the session breathing. It seemed ridiculous at the time, but Ellie did feel calmer afterward.

"I would like to see you again next week. Meanwhile, you are welcome to come to me anytime you need to talk." Dr. Sophia conveyed warmly, placing her hand on Ellie's shoulder.

Ellie thanked Dr. Sophia as she left. Dr. Sophia wasn't at all what Ellie thought she would be. Talking about Angela and Tiffany-Ann was like lifting off a weight. Ellie took a deep breath in and turned to go to her locker. She practically jumped when she realized that the weird boy from that morning was standing beside her.

"Hi, I'm Ellie," she said. She was feeling much braver now that she knew how to breathe.

"I'm Chris. Sorry if I freaked you out earlier at your locker. I can be intense sometimes. Oh my god, you like My Sister Cellophane too?"

he asked excitedly, glancing at the patches on her bag. The transition from serious to goofy seemed abrupt with this guy.

"Yeah! I'm a huge fan!" Ellie responded in surprise. None of the other kids at school appreciated the band's exceptional talent.

"Miles is SO HOT!" he exclaimed, mouth gawking open to amplify how hot he thought the band's singer was. Ellie was taken aback for a moment. She wasn't surprised Chris was gay; she was surprised he was so open about it. She quickly gathered herself. "I KNOW, RIGHT?" she agreed as she jumped up and down. He began jumping with her.

"Hey, do you want to hang out at the mall after school?" he asked. Ellie was excited about a potential friendship but wanted to play it cool.

"Oh my god, yes!" she shouted in response. Okay, not so cool. Oh, well.

"Let's meet outside the gym. Okay, bye!" He waved the same overly-flourished wave as he did earlier. Ellie watched as he walk away, swinging his arms and bouncing on his heels. Yes, Chris was definitely friendship material.

· · · • · • · • · ·

"Hey, Trombone! I heard you got into a little spat yesterday," greeted Nicole, banging mindlessly on the timpani. "Excellent!"

Ellie flushed a bit. She was surprised at how fast the news had traveled. She smiled sheepishly at Nicole and fetched her trombone.

"So, dude, tell me all about it," Nicole continued, "Was there blood and gore spilling everywhere? Did she beg for mercy?" Nicole stared intently at Ellie. "Did you get detention?"

"Actually, no. Mr. Martinez sent the other girl to his office."

"Did he, now?" Nicole asked with a wink.

With all the excitement, Ellie never stopped to think about how lucky she was that she didn't get into trouble. She had already been to see Principal Martinez once. He had warned her about further disruptions. Why did he let her off so easily?

"Let's start from the beginning, nice and lively, now," Mr. Schwartz commanded as he walked into the room, "and try not to make a mockery out of Holst."

*"Okay, I have to focus,"* thought Ellie as the melody of Holst's March began to swirl around her. Except focusing proved entirely impossible. Ellie's new-found confidence began to cave into doubt. What was going on? She started to lose track of all the strange events happening in her life over the past few days. Ellie knew the voice in the locker had something to do with it, but how? She would have to try conversing with her locker. Yes, because that's a completely normal thing to do. The other kids would hear her and double down on the bullying, which had finally started to wane for the first time in her life. She needed to figure out how to investigate her locker in private.

"Dude, you're on the wrong part," Nicole whispered behind her.

Oh no, she made a mockery out of Holst.

Ellie frantically tried to find her place, glancing at Paul's stand to see what section he was on. She didn't think it was possible to grimace while playing the trombone, but Paul managed it anyway. Ellie remembered Dr. Sophia's calming presence. She drew in a deep breath and exhaled out slowly, allowing her to refocus on the moment. She connected with the music and found her place again, resolving to keep her head in the present until she could properly mull over the week's events.

# Chapter 4

# Embrace Your Power

After school, Ellie waited for Chris outside the gym as planned. She checked her watch repeatedly. He probably wouldn't show. Maybe it was even a trap. Yes, someone put him up to it. All the bullies in all the world were about to converge on that exact...oh, wait...there was Chris, smiling and waving his goofy wave, bobbing up and down as he walked.

Their outing at the mall was a fantastic diversion for Ellie. She and Chris hit the food court, tried on ridiculous clothes, and invented stories for random strangers.

"See this guy?" Chris began, "He collects unicorn figurines he hides from his wife. But what he doesn't know is that she, too, hides a unicorn collection."

Ellie laughed so hard she snorted out her drink.

"Okay, this lady here is clearly a hoarder," he continued, "Those shopping bags are full of clothes for her twenty cats."

"Oh, this guy here," Ellie chimed in, pointing to an unsuspecting gentleman, "he's got bodies in his basement."

Chris looked at her with a startled but amused expression. "Whoa, girl, you are dark." At first, Ellie thought she had created a social faux pas, but Chris just laughed about it. Ellie sighed with relief and allowed herself to relax a bit more. She didn't let her guard down too often.

Ellie learned a lot about Chris on that first of what would be many outings together. He was a sophomore who danced alone in his room. He loved animals and walking on the beach at night. He missed his brother, who had just left for college. Most importantly, Ellie learned that she could be herself, truly herself, around him. There was a part of Ellie that she kept carefully hidden: a daring and dark sense of humor she thought no one else could possibly understand. She would be locked away if people knew what she was thinking half the time. That hidden voice came out around Chris. Not only did he embrace her weirdness, he found it funny.

Ellie wanted to confide in Chris about the locker but didn't want to risk alienating her new friend so soon. She was aching to tell someone. The mystery occupied her every thought. She would have to fake a trip to the bathroom during class tomorrow to have some alone time with her locker. Because that's normal.

· · • · • · • · ·

Ellie decided to make her move during band. Mr. Schwartz would be the teacher least likely to notice a prolonged bathroom break. The day progressed at a snail's pace in anticipation. The locker popped open that morning as soon as Ellie reached it. The light inside danced around as if it were happy to see her. It occurred to Ellie that this might terrify other people, but she was not like other people. "I'll be back soon," she told the light show as it zoomed around. She barely noticed Olivia's snarl during math. She was so preoccupied with the locker that she even made mistakes in astronomy.

By band time, Ellie was a nervous wreck. When Nicole nodded at her, Ellie screamed, "Hi!" much too loudly. Nicole momentarily stopped banging her drum to give Ellie a scrutinizing look, then resumed her drumming.

Ellie waited for Mr. Schwartz to call for the woodwinds to rehearse before asking for the bathroom pass. She tried her best not to run to her locker, but anxiety had kicked in strongly by that point. Thankfully no one else was in the hallway. The locker popped open to greet her. She inhaled a long, slow breath. "Hi, um, locker?" she eked out, feeling hopeful and silly.

"Embrace your power," replied the voice, now even stronger but still wavering. Ellie stuck her head right up to the locker to hear it better.

"Am I hurting people?" she asked.

"Embrace your power," the voice repeated.

Ellie tried again. "What power? What am I doing?" She was starting to feel discouraged. "Can you hear me?"

"Embrace your power."

Principal Martinez turned the corner and headed towards Ellie. She panicked, grabbing the first book out of her locker.

"Shouldn't you be in class, Eleanor?" he asked.

"Yes, Principal Martinez. I just forgot my history book," she answered, holding up her math book. He eyed her quizzically.

"Okay, well, be on your way, then," he urged, walking back towards his office.

Ellie put her math book back in the locker. But when she tried to close it, it forced itself back open. The voice spoke once more:

"It was your power."

The words rang out strong, echoing through Ellie's brain. The locker slammed shut. Ellie stood still, mouth agape. *"It was your power."* The words repeated in Ellie's head as she darted back to the band room. *"What power? The bookshelf falling on Olivia? My backpack hitting Angela?"* Ellie feared she already knew. And the voice...it answered her! Ellie returned to the band room, gave the pass to Mr. Schwartz, and took her seat.

Ellie felt the need to talk to Dr. Sophia again immediately. She knew she couldn't tell her about the locker, but she longed for the feeling of warmth and compassion. She decided to head to the counselor's office after band to see if there was an open appointment. As it happened, Dr. Sophia was heading toward her office when Ellie arrived.

"Eleanor McNeil. Lovely to see you! Why, you look a bit disheveled. Would you like to come in?" offered Dr. Sophia. A wave of relief washed over Ellie. They entered the office, Ellie taking a seat while Dr. Sophia lunged for the candy bowl.

"What's up?" asked Dr. Sophia. Ellie didn't know where to begin. How much should she confess? She started slowly.

"Well, that girl Olivia is still teasing me in math," she began tentatively.

"Is she now?" commented Dr. Sophia, munching on candy. Ellie was a bit taken aback by this behavior.

"Yes," Ellie replied hesitantly, "I've been trying to follow your advice and breathe, but it's really hard sometimes."

"Are you still feeling dizzy spells?" Dr. Sophia asked, now staring intently at Ellie. Ellie tried to remember when she told Dr. Sophia about the dizzy spells. She unloaded a lot during their first meeting, but she didn't remember mentioning that part. Something was starting to feel off.

"Are things feeling out of control?" continued Dr. Sophia, "What about things you don't realize are happening? Any unexplained phenomena?" The questions were coming so fast that Ellie was getting confused. Finally, Dr. Sophia got up from her chair and stared directly into Ellie's face. "Any unusual activity from your locker?"

"Yes!" Ellie confessed, in a total state of confusion.

"I KNEW IT!" screamed Dr. Sophia. Except it was no longer Dr. Sophia standing before her, it was Nicole.

"What? What the... WHAT?" stammered Ellie.

"I knew I couldn't be the only one! As soon as I saw you...I just knew the locker gave you magic powers, too!" shouted Nicole excitedly.

"Only one what? What is happening?"

"The locker, Ellie! The ball of light! Shapeshifting into other people! It's all because of the magic locker!" Nicole exclaimed. Nicole magically transformed her appearance into Dr. Sophia, then back to herself again. Ellie began to understand as the shock of seeing Nicole transform into Dr. Sophia wore off. Ellie got up, and the two paced around the office.

"The locker. A magic locker." Yes, Ellie was starting to process it all. "So, I'm turning into other people? How? How did I knock over an entire bookshelf and no one notice?"

Nicole stopped pacing. "You what?"

"A bookcase fell, almost hitting Olivia Hurley while she was teasing me. I hit Angela Anders with my backpack," explained Ellie, "I think. I don't know. I don't remember it. It happened so fast. It was all blurry."

"When I first got my power, I didn't realize what was happening either. Everything kind of blurred. I would look down and see my legs and feet didn't look like mine. My face would look slightly different whenever I saw myself in a mirror. Then I started to focus on transforming into a specific person. At first, I could only transform, like, one body part... an arm or my face. Eventually, I could shapeshift instantly into whoever I wanted. It took a while, though." Nicole had a sudden idea. Ellie could practically see a lightbulb appear over her head. "Ellie, have you noticed any differences in your appearance at all?"

"Not that I know of," Ellie replied. She recalled looking in the mirror that morning. Nope, it was the same old, boring Ellie with unwieldy hair looking back at her.

"Maybe your power isn't shapeshifting. Maybe the magic locker gave you something else!" Nicole exclaimed. They heard a noise outside the door. "Dude, look, we need to get out of here. Let's go to my house after school, and we'll figure it out."

· · · · ●·●·●·· ·

When the dismissal bell rang, Ellie headed to her magic locker. It popped open to greet her once again. "I'm on to you," Ellie whispered to it giddily.

"Embrace your power," it answered, light bouncing around the left side.

"And what might that power be?" asked Ellie. The light kept bouncing. "Silent treatment, huh? Okay!" Ellie's annoyance at the voice could not dampen her excitement for hanging out with Nicole. She had so many questions for her!

Ellie met Nicole at the school's entrance. They chatted excitedly as they walked to Nicole's house, careful not to divulge too much until the coast was clear. There were fewer kids within earshot once they got past the old abandoned warehouse behind the school, and their talk became less guarded.

"How long have you been able to do it?" Ellie asked Nicole.

"Since freshman year. I had just moved here and was a lot shyer then. With a last name like 'Faisal', the other kids teased me from the start. That locker was my only friend!" She added the last part jokingly, but

Ellie sensed sadness in Nicole's reminiscing. "Anyway, I can't wait to see what you can do!"

"Not without me, you won't," said a voice from behind them. Both girls jumped and spun around. Chris was standing behind them, smirking. "Hey, Ellie! You're Nicole, right? I'm Chris."

"Uh. Yeah. Hi. Um, we were just discussing a school project we're doing." Ellie's explanation sounded as bad of a lie as it was. Chris rolled his eyes.

"If by 'school project' you mean the magic locker, then yes. I heard *everything*." The way Chris empathized *"everything"* made Ellie very suspicious.

"What do you mean *'everything'*?" she asked.

"The locker gave me super-senses. I see, taste, smell, and hear everything amplified. It's a curse, really," he explained, somewhat casually.

Ellie stared at Chris in shock. A sly smile spread across Nicole's face.

"Welp, you have to come with us, then," she demanded, putting her arm around Chris' shoulder. The result was comical, considering he was a foot taller than her. Nicole quickly looked around to see if anyone was watching, then transformed into the girls' basketball captain, the very tall Latisha Adams, to even out their heights.

Nicole turned back into herself as they reached her house. She led them around to a back door, which opened to a large basement. The room was filled with all kinds of instruments, amps, and equipment, with a large drum set in the center. The walls were covered in posters of bands Ellie did not know. Several anarchy symbols were spray painted on the floor. Old couches and abandoned furniture were placed haphazardly throughout the room. Ellie had never been in such a fantastic room before. She smiled to herself, thinking what her mother's reaction would be.

"Beer?" Nicole offered, opening a mini fridge. Ellie froze. She had only tried small amounts of alcohol under her parents' strict supervision. She didn't want to seem uncool but wasn't ready for a beer.

"Kidding! I have soda and OJ." Nicole laughed. Ellie was relieved. She and Chris grabbed sodas and sat down on a couch covered with a brightly-colored crocheted blanket.

Ellie had planned to wait for Nicole to start the conversation but couldn't wait a moment longer. "Have you been Dr. Sophia this whole time?"

"No, I followed you out of the band room," Nicole explained, "You looked upset. When I saw you at your locker, I thought maybe you were like me."

"I didn't see you at my locker," claimed Ellie.

"Actually, you did," Nicole confessed, morphing into Principal Martinez with a wink, then back to herself. "Anyway, I thought I would become Dr. Sophia to try to pull you into her office so we could talk privately, but you were already there."

"You can become the principal?" asked Chris in awe.

"I can become anyone," boasted Nicole, transforming into Chris.

"Okay, that is just off-putting," he whined.

"Sorry," said Nicole, transforming back into herself. "The weird thing is, that isn't the same locker I had, so I remained as Dr. Sophia until I was sure."

"I thought the same," added Chris, turning to face Ellie, "When I heard the scuffle between you and Angela Anders, I immediately headed towards my freshman locker to see if it had given another person powers."

"What number was your locker?" asked Ellie.

"G23," Chris replied, turning to Nicole, "What about yours?"

"G48," she answered.

Ellie thought about it for a moment. "So, it chose us," she concluded, "But my power isn't shapeshifting or super-senses. How do I figure out what's happening?"

"Mine came about slowly," began Chris, "I saw a faint light in my locker. A couple of days later, food started tasting differently. I had trouble studying because I could hear the downstairs television like it was right next to me. As the light in the locker became brighter, my senses became stronger. What exactly has happened to you so far?"

Ellie recounted the incidents with Angela and Olivia with as much detail as possible.

"Hmmm. Super strength?" suggested Chris.

"Oh, Dude!" Nicole shouted excitedly, pointing to an old, sturdy-looking table. "Lift that table! It's super heavy!"

Ellie put her hands under the table to try to lift it, carefully at first to not send it flying with her super-strength. When it didn't budge, she tried lifting it with all of her might. Nope, not super-strength.

"Okay, well, are there any other weird things happening?" asked Chris.

Ellie thought about it. "Did either of your lockers pop open for you?" The other two shook their heads. "Okay, well, my locker pops open by itself."

"Woh! That is so cool!" exclaimed Nicole.

"What are you thinking about when that happens?" asked Chris.

"I was worried I wouldn't remember the combination. I'm terrible with numbers, and everyone makes fun of me when I look at my note with the combination written on it," replied Ellie.

Chris sat pensively for several minutes while Nicole entertained Ellie by transforming into different teachers.

"Ellie," began Chris, still in deep concentration, "your backpack *moved* without you realizing, the bookshelf *moved* without you near it, and your locker *moved* without you touching it."

"Yes," confirmed Ellie, "do you think I could have done those things subconsciously, like, in my mind?" Ellie felt ridiculous even suggesting it.

"It's called telekinesis," explained Chris. "The ability to move objects without touching them. " The girls stared at him blankly. He shrugged, adding, "You control objects with your mind. After I got super-senses, I started to read a lot of comic books."

"Oh WOW!" screamed Nicole, transforming from Mr. Schwartz back into herself, "Ellie! Move the table with *brain power*!"

Ellie looked at them doubtfully, but they were both nodding in encouragement. Ellie concentrated on the table, scrunching up her eyes. It didn't budge. She tried to focus harder. Still not moving. She held out her arms with Chris-like flourish, hoping that would somehow help. That didn't work either. She inhaled a long, slow breath, closed her eyes, relaxed her mind, and visualized the table gliding across the floor. She slowly opened her eyes.

Nothing.

Ellie looked at her friends. They looked disappointed. *"Here it comes,"* she thought. *"I'm a failure. They hate me now. I don't deserve any friends anyway. Tiffany-Ann was right. I'm just a loser. Even Angela turned against me."*

Ellie's thoughts were interrupted by the sound of creaking and her friends erupting with joy. The table was floating three feet in the air.

# Chapter 5

# Sunshine

That night, Ellie sat on her bed and surveyed the contents on her desk. *"Okay, telekinesis. Move things with my mind."* She decided to focus on lifting the stapler. It didn't move. How could she lift a table but not a stapler? She thought about Chris' question regarding what she was thinking about when her locker opened. What was she thinking about when she lifted the table? Tiffany-Ann's torment: Angela's betrayal. Ellie's fear and anger triggered the telekinesis. Concentrating once again on the stapler, Ellie remembered Tiffany-Ann chasing her around the playground in second grade, threatening to kick her ass while all the other kids watched. The stapler shot upwards, hit the mobile of the solar system on the ceiling, then crashed down to the floor.

"Ellie? Is everything all right up there?" called her mother.

"Yes, Mom, just getting ready for bed," Ellie responded. She'd have to stop for now. Ellie wasn't ready to tell her parents her secret yet. She wanted to be able to control her power first. Plus, she wasn't ready to admit that she could have seriously hurt Olivia Hurley: to her parents, or to herself. But if anyone deserved it, Olivia sure did.

Ellie was shocked by her own thought. She had been teased and bullied her entire life but had never thought about harming someone before. Chris had said he never hit anyone back. Ellie vowed not to let Olivia push her buttons like that again. She put her glasses on the nightstand, set her alarm, and slowly drifted into a fitful sleep.

She dreamed of the magic locker, surrounded by swirling lights of different colors. She sang a My Sister Cellophane song and danced with the lights. The locker opened slowly, sucking her in with an explosion of gorgeous blues, greens, and pinks resembling space. It was not scary; it was calling her home.

· · · ● · ● · · ·

The next morning, Ellie woke with an enthusiasm for school she had never felt before. She always loved learning but never really had friends. Sure, there were the kids in band, but she never really hung out with them outside of school functions. There was a bond between her, Chris, and Nicole. Ellie felt ashamed that she had questioned their friendship the previous day when she failed to lift the table. Trust no longer came naturally to her after years of bullying. Still, Ellie did not want to let her past punish her friends. Friends. The word made her jubilant.

Ellie practically skipped into the school. Principal Martinez was giving his daily pep talk over the loudspeaker, something about playing to your strengths in order to score in the game of life. Chris and Nicole were waiting for her at her locker, Chris waving his goofy wave in his oversized blazer and Nicole sporting her half-cocked grin, drumming on the locker next to Ellie's. The anarchy symbol on Nicole's arm was blue today. They were gleeful when Ellie's locker popped open by itself as she approached.

"Dude, that is so epic!" Nicole said enthusiastically.

"Okay, bye!" Chris waved and darted away.

"Does he always leave so abruptly?" asked Nicole.

"Pretty much, yeah," laughed Ellie. She found it endearing.

Nicole shrugged. "That's cool. A bit dramatic, but cool. See you in band," she said, briefly turning her face into Mr. Schwartz's. Ellie looked around nervously, but Nicole was careful enough to only be facing Ellie. Nicole walked down the hallway with a vigorous swagger, drumsticks in her back pocket. One kid shouted "terrorist" at her, but Nicole kept walking, flipping him off as she passed. Ellie wished she could handle situations like that with Nicole's attitude. Ellie hung up her hoodie and grabbed her math book. As the locker was shutting, she heard the voice ring out.

"Ahhhh, I feel it. I feel your power."

It sounded stronger and more sinister than before. Ellie tried to reopen the locker, but the lock wouldn't move. The bell rang. Ellie ran for math class and arrived sweaty and disheveled but on time. This time she didn't care. Something about the voice sounded different than before.

"Pop quiz time," announced Mrs. Canter. The class groaned.

*"I bet you'll fail, Smelly Ellie."*

Olivia was relentless.

*"You're such a dumbass."*

Ellie took the quiz papers being handed down the rows from the boy in front of her. She took one, then turned to pass them to Olivia, trying her best to channel Nicole's carefree attitude.

Olivia sported her infamous sneer. "You better watch your back because I'm coming for you," she taunted under her breath. Ellie felt pure terror. Olivia had been insulting Ellie for weeks, but this was a direct threat. Ellie dropped the papers, memories of Tiffany-Ann Trombley's abuse flooding her brain. The entire class laughed as she hurried to pick them all up.

"What's the problem, Ms. McNeil?" Mrs. Canter asked sternly.

"Nothing, Mrs. Canter," replied Ellie, handing the papers to Olivia, who gave her a smug look.

The class settled down and began the quiz. Ellie was fuming. Then she had an idea. She focused her anger on moving Olivia's pencil. Immediately she heard furious scratching behind her.

"What the hell?" questioned a surprised Olivia. Ellie stifled a giggle. She focused once more. The pencil flew past Ellie's feet and rolled toward Mrs. Canter's desk. The teacher looked annoyed as Olivia fetched it. Ellie was feeling more confident now. Olivia sat back down. Ellie could sense her frustration. Ellie waited a few minutes, then focused her attention on the pencil once again. It flew over Ellie's head and hit the boy in front of her. He turned around, startled. Olivia went to retrieve her pencil, her signature sneer gone.

"Ms. Hurley, please gain control of your pencil," demanded Mrs. Canter. The class snickered. Now it was time for the finishing move.

Ellie channeled all her anger toward the pencil. Suddenly, Olivia ran down the classroom aisle, pencil leading the way, clutched in her hand. The class erupted in laughter.

"Olivia Hurley, to the principal's office!" Mrs. Canter's voice boomed over the laughter, "Everyone else, quiet down!"

Ellie released the pencil from her mind. Olivia's arm went down like a puppet. She glared at Ellie as she slumped out the door. By the end of math, Ellie was still very pleased with herself. She wondered why the voice in her locker had sounded strange to her at all.

"Possessed pencil, huh?" Chris smirked, meeting up with Ellie in the hallway.

"You could hear that?" asked a shocked Ellie.

"Yeah, I can hear miles away. But in school, I have to concentrate to zero in on the area I want to hear. Too much noise."

"Wow, that's amazing!"

"Okay, bye!" he waved and bounced away.

When Ellie reached her locker, she was a bit worried, but it decided to pop open. Phew.

"Did you see that?" she proudly whispered to the voice.

"Yesssssssss," the voice hissed back, "Your power is growing. I can taste it."

Ellie saw Angela Anders heading down the hallway. She stopped abruptly and changed course to avoid Ellie.

"Doooooo it," the voice urged. Ellie concentrated on Angela's moment of betrayal. Suddenly, Angela fell to the floor as if her feet had been swept out from under her. The hallway filled with laughter.

"Ahhhhhhh," savored the voice. The light bounced around approvingly.

"Nicely done," praised Nicole. Ellie hadn't even noticed her approach with all the commotion.

"Thanks," she gushed.

"The whole school is talking about Olivia Hurley's strange behavior in class today. I assume you had something to do with that?"

Ellie smiled triumphantly.

"Oh, dude, I am so proud of you! See you later!"

Ellie noticed her locker was shut. She wasn't sure when it happened, but she had the book she needed anyway. She shrugged it off and headed to class. When she passed Dr. Sophia's office, Ellie remembered that she never actually had her follow-up appointment with the real Dr. Sophia. She quickly arranged an appointment for the following day.

· · • • • • • • · ·

After school, the trio headed to Nicole's house again. Chris and Nicole whooped and laughed as Ellie recounted the possessed pencil incident, as they were now calling it.

"I wish I could've seen that," laughed Nicole as they entered the basement, "I am so sick of jerks like Olivia Hurley! Thankfully I only have one more year left. Then I'm off to tour the world!" Nicole took a seat at her drum set and played an aggressive beat. Ellie noticed a sticker on the snare drum that read "Payne HS."

"Did Mr. Schwartz let you borrow that?" Ellie asked.

"I can *borrow* whatever I want when I *am* Mr. Schwartz!" Nicole shouted over her drum playing, turning herself into the band director. Inwardly, Ellie was shocked but tried to play it cool. Chris decided to change the subject.

"How were you able to focus your telekinesis with Olivia today?" he asked Ellie.

"Well, I was getting really angry and flustered until I decided to focus on the pencil. At first, I couldn't control it at all. The more scared I got about Olivia's threat, the more control I seemed to gain over it."

"Interesting," said Chris. Ellie thought he was a Dr. Sophia-in-the-making. "Have you tried using other emotions?"

"Not really," she answered, "It seems to be fueled by fear or anger."

"I had been bullied by Austin Cole for years." Chris started, his usual cheerful demeanor turning somber. "He would call me a fag, steal my shoes, put my head in a toilet. Once, he even hit me in the stomach during gym, claiming it was an accident. When I got my power, the first thing I noticed was being able to hear him and his squad coming from far away. I was able to avoid him by always knowing where he was."

"Dude! Same here!" exclaimed Nicole, transforming from Principal Martinez back into herself, "I had just moved here, and kids were like, 'terrorist this and terrorist that' 'where's your bomb hidden,' 'go back to where you came from.' So, I started roaming the halls as other people." Nicole seemed different to Ellie at that moment. Nicole always seemed so confident, like nothing could ever hurt her. Seeing her friend so vulnerable made Ellie sad. She couldn't believe anyone could see Nicole as anything other than the most awesome human on the planet. Chris seemed like the type of guy who always had a target on his back, but his story upset Ellie nonetheless. Thinking about it is one thing, hearing it straight from his mouth was heartbreaking.

"So, the magic locker chooses kids who are bullied," concluded Ellie. Another thought had been circulating her mind that day. "Chris, you're a sophomore. Nicole: junior. I'm a freshman. Do you think there's a senior at school who has a magic power?"

"I was wondering that," agreed Chris, "but I haven't seen or heard anything strange happening. I've been trying to focus more. But like I said, there's a lot of noise in school."

"Well, we should probably keep a lookout just in case. There may be others we don't know about," added Ellie. Nicole looked pensive as she turned into Austin Cole, Dr. Sophia, a convenience store worker, Olivia Hurley, then back to Austin Cole.

Another thing had been bothering Ellie. "Do you think we lose our powers when we graduate?" she asked. Nicole stopped transforming, frozen as herself. "I mean, if we leave and are too far from the locker? And if the locker gives someone powers every year, then wouldn't there be hundreds of magic users around? Wouldn't people have noticed?"

"I don't want to go through life like this," confessed Chris, "always knowing everything about everyone. I hear all their secrets. Things I don't want to know." He shuddered, then composed himself, "Everything I taste, smell. It's overpowering." It had never occurred to Ellie that super-senses might be hard to live with. She was glad to have telekinesis instead. No wonder Chris was so thin. Eating must be a challenge for him. She decided not to say anything that might make him feel bad, so all she managed to say was, "That sucks, dude." No one ever accused Ellie of being eloquent. No matter, Chris nodded appreciatively anyway.

· · • • · • • • · ·

The next morning Ellie woke up with a smile on her face. She danced around her room to the new My Sister Cellophane song while she got ready for school. The solar system hanging from her ceiling seemed to dance along with her. It was the first track released from MSC's upcoming album. The song was called "Sunshine," but the lyrics reflected the band's normal doom and gloom. Ellie thrived on the irony. The entire album was due for release, but she wasn't sure when. The band was being particularly secretive about it. Ellie kept an eye on their social media channels like a hawk, savoring every clue the band dropped about it. They had already posted images of Henry the Eighth (thankfully, fans posted who he was in the comments as Ellie did not know who he was), a computer keyboard, a drawing of the sun (now thought to be a hint to the first track), and a white square with the name "Holst" in the middle in black. Ellie was enthralled by this last clue since they were practicing Holst's March in concert band. She couldn't find any other significance to "Holst" on the internet, so she assumed it meant the composer.

Ellie was having a great morning. She aced her English test, saw photos from the Hubble Telescope during astronomy, and, best of all, endured far fewer insults from the other students. She wished she hadn't booked the appointment with Dr. Sophia. She felt great and didn't want the session to bring her down. But being in high school meant becoming an adult, so Ellie decided to keep her appointment. It was the mature thing to do.

"Good morning, Ellie. Nice to see you again," greeted Dr. Sophia. Today she was wearing a deep red A-line dress with impossibly high heels. Ellie wondered how she could walk in them without falling. Her mother's shoe choices were far more sensible.

Ellie took a seat, surveying Dr. Sophia's actions. The counselor was calm, composed, and not lunging at the candy bowl. Okay, she most likely wasn't Nicole in disguise. The last thing Ellie wanted was for her friend to hear all her faults.

"How is everything?" asked Dr. Sophia.

*"Well, my locker gave me superpowers; I lifted a table with my mind, tormented Olivia and Angela; oh, and the voice I'm hearing is getting stronger, and it converses with me now, sometimes I think it's menacing,"* thought Ellie. Nope, still not ready.

"Pretty good, actually. I made some friends!" she answered instead. She studied Dr. Sophia's reaction, wondering if it still might be Nicole playing a trick on her. She decided it was the real doctor, so she told her a bit about Chris and Nicole.

"That's good to hear, Ellie," replied the counselor, in the warm, reassuring tone that put Ellie at ease during their first session. "How is your schoolwork going?"

"Okay. I'm doing well mostly, but math is mind-numbingly difficult for me." Ellie shuddered, thinking about math. She just kept telling herself she wouldn't need it once she graduated. It was her only way to cope.

"Tell me about that. Is your relationship with Olivia Hurley impacting your studies?" questioned Dr. Sophia.

"I don't think so. I've never been great at math," Ellie answered. It was the truth, but Ellie couldn't help thinking about her dipping history grade the year she sat next to Tiffany-Ann Trombley. Did Tiffany-Ann's constant insults affect Ellie's grade?

"I heard Olivia had quite the adventure yesterday," the counselor continued, staring so intently at Ellie that she felt like she could see her soul, "How did that make you feel?"

*"Great! Fantastic! Elated! I hope they commit her for eternity!"* Wait, did she say that out loud? Nope, the counselor was still waiting for her to speak.

"It was a relief they weren't laughing at me for once. I could join in." Oh no, was that too honest? Ellie was worried the counselor would discover the deep, dark ball of revenge growing within her. They would figure out how to take her magic power away, and she would go back to being mocked and friendless. Or worse, maybe *she* would be the one committed forever.

"Thank you for your honesty, Ellie. Sometimes the truth can be difficult to admit. But I promise it will help you grow." Dr. Sophia always said the right thing. Dr. Sophia guided Ellie through more breathing exercises. Ellie left the session feeling even better than before.

Chris and Nicole were waiting for Ellie at her locker. Ellie noticed Olivia on the far side of the hallway. With a quick focus on revenge, Ellie knocked Olivia's books down to the floor. As luck would have it, Angela was right next to Olivia. Olivia punched a very confused Angela on the arm, "Watch it, loser!" Olivia shouted at her. Nicole, Chris, and Ellie laughed uncontrollably. Angela simply walked away, completely baffled at what had just happened.

"Two for one! Nice!" praised Nicole. The anarchy symbol was green today. Ellie felt jubilated. This day could not get any better.

"I've listened to 'Sunshine,' like, a hundred times already!" exclaimed Chris.

"I know, right? It's fantastic!" Ellie agreed.

"I like it, too!" joined Nicole, "But I still like harder stuff like Drone Monkey." She winked and headed to her next class.

Chris and Ellie headed down the other way together.

"What do you think of the clues so far?" asked Ellie.

"I don't know. I was thinking it might be their influences or something. Maybe the keyboard means it's going to be electronica or something," he suggested.

"Maybe they have a new keyboard player?" she proposed. They laughed together. MSC was notorious for replacing keyboardists.

"Maybe a new keyboardist named Holst!" Chris was excited by the idea. A quick search on their phones revealed nothing about keyboardists named Holst. "I'll dig deeper during study hall. Well, bye!"

Ellie continued down the hallway to English class, imagining a keyboardist named Holst with the stature of Henry the Eighth, sun shining brightly behind him.

# Chapter 6

## Witches & Genies

Over the next few days, Ellie concentrated on honing her power. She could move both light and heavy objects with equal ease. She discovered that she could move an object without having to see it if she already knew where it was. Although Chris could see and hear for miles, Ellie could only move objects from about twenty feet away. She hoped to be able to extend her range with more concentrated anger. Between bullies and the news of the world, there was no shortage of fury she could channel. She also noticed the voice inside the locker was getting stronger. Ellie could only extract a few phrases from it, but she was no longer afraid of it. She would have to remember to ask Chris and Nicole about what they heard. With the excitement of practicing their magic, talk of the locker itself had become less prominent.

One delightful morning, Ellie decided to skip to school. She just swept the teasing aside. Literally. Anyone who mocked her found themselves on the ground. Ellie strode towards her locker, trying to imitate Nicole's swagger.

"Dude, what's wrong with your leg? Are you hurt?" asked a concerned Nicole. Ellie flushed red. Okay, work on swagger later.

"Nope, good as gold!" Ellie answered, changing her gait back to normal as she approached her friend. Ellie happily noted Nicole's anarchy symbol was purple today. Her favorite color.

The locker popped open, allowing Ellie to retrieve her astronomy book, "Good morning, locker!" she greeted.

"Okay, you're weird. See you in band!" Nicole laughed. Ellie studied her movements. Damn, that was some good swagger.

"Good morning, Eleanor," the voice answered, "Your power is strong now. It's time to deal with Olivia Hurley."

"Deal with?" repeated Ellie. The light bounced around, bright as ever. The locker slammed shut. "Deal with," whispered Ellie. The locker wanted her to punish Olivia more than she already had? Ellie had embarrassed Olivia in front of math class, tripped her multiple times in the hallway, and made it impossible for Olivia to keep hold of her books. It was glorious. But what more could Ellie do?

She thought about this through science class. When Mr. Joshi called on her, she wasn't paying any attention.

"Uh, Mars?" she answered tentatively.

"Eleanor, the question was which star is brightest in the Northern Hemisphere," the teacher said sternly.

"Mars can be pretty bright," replied Ellie flippantly. What was wrong with her? She had never talked back to a teacher before. Mr. Joshi looked at her pensively. Ellie froze.

"I suggest you focus on your studies, Eleanor. Jayden, can you tell me which star is the brightest in the Northern Hemisphere?"

Ellie exhaled slowly in relief. She suspected Mr. Joshi let her off with a warning because she hadn't caused trouble in his class before. Ellie never expected balancing super-powers with schoolwork would be so difficult. She would have to send a strongly worded email to the movie industry.

"Yo, how goes it?" Nicole shouted over her drumming as Ellie entered the band room.

"Well, I said Mars was a star in science class, so it's been better," Ellie answered, retrieving her trombone. Paul nodded to her as she took her seat and began to warm up.

"Hey, have you seen the new kid yet?" asked Nicole, "he's British!"

Ellie whipped around in excitement. "A British guy! Here?"

"Yeah, he's pretty cute, too," Nicole said with a wink. Ellie imagined the new student looking like MSC's bass player, Graham Taylor. What else could he possibly look like?

Nicole leaned in and whispered, "Hey, I got a hold of some firecrackers. I thought it would be fun to explode them in the air with your power." She had a mischievous gleam in her eye. Ellie smiled in return, wondering where Nicole may have obtained such items.

· · · ● · ● · · · ·

"OH MY GOD, DID YOU SEE THE NEW BRITISH GUY?"
screamed Chris, grabbing Ellie's arm in the hallway. She practically
jumped a mile in surprise. She supposed super-senses caused him to
have super-stealth as well.

"Not yet," laughed Ellie.

"We'll have to befriend him before the popular kids get him," schemed
Chris. Ellie felt this was a solid plan.

"What grade is he in?"

"Sophomore! He's in my English class! His name is Simon, and he's
dreamy!" Chris swooned. Ellie once again pictured Graham Taylor
and swooned along with Chris.

"I almost forgot...did you see the new MSC clue?" Chris asked, pulling
out his phone.

"What? No! How did I miss it?" Ellie gasped, looking at Chris' phone.
A photo of Mars was posted on MSC's website. Ellie was taken aback.
It was a strange coincidence. "Wow, I wasn't paying attention in
science today, and I just blurted out 'Mars' since I didn't know what
the question was."

"You're in tune with Graham," teased Chris. Ellie giggled ridiculously.

*"Dork"*

The assailant fell to the ground. Ellie and Chris laughed
uncontrollably.

· · · · ● · ● · · ·

As it turned out, exploding firecrackers in the air was much more enjoyable than Ellie had imagined. Nicole would light them, then Ellie flew them into the air one by one, naming every kid that ever made fun of her. They had gone to the abandoned warehouse behind the school for some privacy. When they ran out of firecrackers, Chris played MSC tunes on his phone. The trio danced and joked. Chris tried to dip Ellie and Nicole together, but they all just ended up falling on the ground laughing.

"I'm so happy we found each other," said Chris.

"I know! And you guys are so cool!" exclaimed Nicole. Cool? Nicole thought Ellie was cool? Ellie was elated.

"That locker changed my life," added Ellie.

"Thank you bouncing ball of light!" proclaimed Chris, saluting the air with an exaggerated flourish.

"That was dramatic," laughed Ellie. "But seriously, where do you think the magic comes from?"

"Space," answered Chris sincerely, "It seems sentient. I imagine that's what life on other planets is like. Everyone's a ball of light."

"I think it might be a Jinn," Nicole answered, as serious as Ellie had ever heard her.

"A what?" asked Ellie and Chris simultaneously.

"A Jinn," Nicole repeated, "a genie," she explained, rolling her eyes. Her friends' faces started looking less puzzled. "Jinn are very powerful. One could certainly grant us powers. Although I've never heard of a Jinn turning into light. It's usually animals or something. Still, I try not to abuse my power too much so it won't punish me in the end."

"What do you mean?" asked Ellie.

"Well, Jinn stories are always about wishes backfiring. Like, you wish to look younger, and you become a baby. Or wishing to bring someone back from the dead and they're a zombie who eats your brain." Nicole had clearly thought about this.

"But we didn't wish for this, did we?" Ellie was uncertain. Maybe somewhere in the back of her mind she had. Could the locker read minds?

"I didn't. Not out loud. That's why I think it's a gift, not a test. But still, I try to be careful. People wind up dead with this kind of power." Nicole shuddered.

"Why didn't it ask us for our wish then?" pondered Ellie.

"I don't think it can talk," replied Chris.

I don't think it can talk. The words sent Ellie into shock.

"It talks to me...." Ellie said slowly. The other two looked at her strangely. "The voice. Inside the locker. Neither of you heard a voice?"

"No!" exclaimed Nicole, "What kind of voice? What does it say?"

"It told me to embrace my power," Ellie looked frantically between her friends as their eyes widened. She didn't want them to be afraid of her. "It knew about the possessed pencil incident. Um, and...it told me that Olivia Hurley needed to be dealt with." The last part rolled out of her uncontrollably. Ellie was starting to think the voice's command was more nefarious than she thought. *"People wind up dead"* repeated in Ellie's mind.

"Dealt with? Ellie, I don't know if this is an alien, a Jinn, or something else, but be careful," warned Chris.

Ellie turned to Nicole for advice, but her friend was silent, shapeshifting from person to person.

"Why am I the only one that can hear it?" Ellie questioned desperately.

"What does it sound like?" Chris asked.

"Well, at first, it was faint and crackly. It grew stronger as the light grew stronger, as I grew stronger. Now she talks to me. I thought she was like a Fairy Godmother to guide me, but sometimes she's more like an Evil Witch. It can be scary sometimes," Ellie decided not to hold back. She would have to trust her friends.

"A witch," Chris repeated, "maybe it's a witch."

"But why would she manifest now, only to me?" wondered Ellie.

"I don't know. Maybe she's gotten stronger with each of us, drawing from our power, and can only now talk?" suggested Chris.

"Does that mean it might become something other than a ball of light? Like a person?" asked Ellie. She glanced at Nicole, who was transforming even more rapidly. Ellie found it very distracting. She wished Nicole would focus.

"I don't know. I wish we knew if there are more of us at school. If we knew when it began, we could tell if it's getting stronger with each power granted. But in all this time, I've heard nothing," Chris seemed frustrated.

"Too bad none of us can make people talk. We could find out from Dr. Sophia if she's encountered any other magical students," commented Ellie.

"I can do that," Nicole said abruptly, transforming into Dr. Sophia's form.

"You can't just pretend to be the counselor," argued Ellie, "You'd have to know how to give advice. What people say in there is private." Ellie wondered how many times Nicole may have posed as the counselor during sessions. Would her friend do that?

"I don't need to talk directly to students. I can go in and look in her files," explained Nicole, still looking like Dr. Sophia, "Hopefully, her laptop has facial recognition!"

Ellie considered the ramifications of breaking into Dr. Sophia's office.

"I think you should do it," agreed Chris, "I don't see what other choice we have. I've been watching and listening for over a year now. I've always thought this power was a bit of a curse. And Ellie may be in danger."

This last sentence took Ellie by surprise. Yes, it had occurred to her that the voice could be dangerous, but she didn't take it too seriously. Now she began to wonder. She reflected on old fairy tales of witches and genies.

· · · · • · • · ·

Ah, yes, stories of witches and genies. Princesses locked in towers. Stockholm Syndrome romances. Be warned, Ellie: Prince Charming isn't coming to save you.

# Ellie the Evil

Ellie watched the ball of light dancing inside of her locker. She had been watching it for several minutes, afraid of the questions she must ask.

"Are you a witch?" she finally whispered to it. The other students went about their business, oblivious to the girl talking to her locker. Ellie waited, but the locker gave no response.

"Is there someone else with magic powers here?" she questioned further, then added, "other than me, Chris, and Nicole," to be clear. No genie trickery here. It made no difference. The locker remained silent. Maybe it was time to poke it with the proverbial stick. Ellie leaned in as far as she could go. She didn't want to risk anyone hearing her next question, especially Chris.

"Do you want me to hurt Olivia Hurley?" The question rang out loud in Ellie's mind, despite having barely whispered it. Ellie had feared the answer not only from the locker, but from herself. Ellie waited several more minutes, convincing herself that she could not hurt anyone.

"Yesssssss," the voice replied strongly, "Yesssssss."

"Yes to what?" asked Ellie, filled with anticipation.

"Yes to all. I gave you your power, and I can take it away. Do what you must to keep it." The locker slammed itself shut. Ellie stared momentarily before texting her friends, "It's a witch. There's another student." She deliberately left out the part about Olivia. That was between her and the witch.

"I love My Sister Cellophane. I got to see them at Glastonbury." The words were spoken with a dreamy British accent. Ellie slowly turned away from the locker towards the speaker, an impossibly tall guy with a small but muscular build. His wavy black hair perfectly matched his gorgeous golden skin. But it was his deep, dark brown eyes that put Ellie into a trance. "Hi, I'm Simon. You must be Ellie." Ellie nodded weakly, still lost in those eyes. She slowly started to regain consciousness.

"Yes, hi Simon!" she replied, a little too eagerly. Be cool, Ellie, be cool.

"Chris told me a lot about you," he explained, "I hope I didn't come off as creepy just walking up to you like this."

Ellie laughed a ridiculous laugh and tried to flip back her ponytail. Except it was already back. Awkward. The bell rang as she tried to force a cool and casual response. "No, not creepy at all! Chris told me about you, too. I couldn't wait to meet you!" Was that out loud? Oh no, it was. He smiled. Phew.

"Well, I'll see you later," he said, delicious accent oozing through Ellie's brain. Ellie went to science class, her head in an entirely different kind of space.

· · • • · • • · ·

At the end of the school day, Ellie headed to the band room to retrieve her trombone so she could practice at home over the weekend. She headed to the back storage area and found a girl weeping in the corner. Ellie didn't really know her. She was a new student, a flute player. Ellie's first thought was to let her be and leave. But she just couldn't.

"Hey, what's wrong?" she asked the girl, sitting on the floor next to her.

"Some kids were making fun of my purse," she answered through tears, "I can't help it. We can't afford much, and it was the only one I could find at the thrift store." Her tears poured down hard. The flame in the pit of Ellie's stomach started to burn with fury.

"People make fun of my bag all the time, too," Ellie told her, holding up her old lady backpack, "I put on patches to cover the rips in it."

"Oh, I love your bag!" the girl praised, perking up a bit. Ellie thought the girl was feeling better, but truthfully, Ellie was feeling better, too. Her anger flame was subsiding.

"Well, I love yours. You do you and ignore them," Ellie realized she needed to take her own advice.

"Thanks," replied the girl, getting up and wiping the last of her tears away.

Ellie got up, too, "I'm Ellie, by the way."

"I'm Izzy," she responded. Ellie grabbed her trombone and they both headed towards the door.

"By the way, who was making fun of you?" Ellie asked.

"Olivia Hurley and her friends," answered Izzy with a disgusted look on her face.

The flame rekindled. Ellie dropped her trombone. She started down the hall, "Where is Olivia Hurley?" she demanded. Some students shrugged in shock, but a few pointed towards the gym. Ellie headed towards the gym, her purpose clear and singular. "Olivia Hurley!" she shouted as she entered the gym. A few of Olivia's friends were there. They laughed at Ellie and pointed toward the exit. "Let's see who'll be laughing," thought Ellie. Their mockery simply fueled her power. She spotted Olivia outside, heading towards the field. "Olivia Hurley! Stop right there!" Ellie ordered. Olivia turned around, saw Ellie, and started to laugh.

"Just who do you think you are, Smelly Ellie?" she teased. Her smug demeanor quickly turned to panic as she flew up into the air. She hovered about ten feet up and began to scream. Ellie tried to remain focused. All the years of teasing, bullying, and being chased surfaced, swirling around her in a rage she could no longer control.

"You will NOT make fun of me or anyone else ever again! Do you understand?" she demanded of Olivia. Ellie pushed to raise Olivia higher. Olivia started wobbling around. Ellie's power was waning.

Suddenly, Ellie was tackled down to the ground. She heard the commotion of Olivia falling and her friends rushing around her, but the sound was distant. Ellie looked around in confusion and realized she was at the abandoned warehouse. She adjusted her glasses and noticed that she wasn't alone. Her eyes met with those of a girl she did not know. The girl was on the smaller side but conveyed a calm confidence reminiscent of Nicole. The girl's head was shaved on both sides, with several inches of afro in the middle. Ellie was not scared; this girl was an ally.

"You could have killed Olivia," she explained. "So I brought you here."

"But I thought I was being a hero," Ellie claimed, ashamed and deflated.

"Not today, you're not," answered the girl sadly. Ellie thought she was defending Izzy, but really, she was seeking revenge for herself.

"How did we get here?" questioned Ellie as she started to fully comprehend her current surroundings.

The girl zipped around Ellie, disappearing from one spot, then appearing in another.

"The magic locker! You're the fourth student!" Ellie exclaimed, suddenly much more cheerful. She stood up and saw Chris and Nicole heading toward them. "She's the fourth!" she shouted to them excitedly.

"What do you mean 'the fourth'?" asked the girl, clearly confused.

"The locker! You got your power from your locker freshman year, right?" the girl nodded as Ellie continued, "I just got my powers. I'm a freshman. Chris got his last year. Nicole got hers two years ago, so we've been looking for a senior with powers! You are a senior, right?"

"Yes. You all have powers?" the girl asked.

Chris waved his goofy wave, "Hi, I'm Chris. I have super-senses." He sniffed at the air in some sort of weird demonstration.

"Nicole," Nicole winked as she introduced herself, transforming into the girl. The girl shouted in surprised delight.

"I'm Kat, teleporter," replied Kat, zipping around to demonstrate. They all clapped in amazement.

"I'm Ellie. Telekinesis. And apparently, I've just made a huge mistake," Ellie confessed.

"What happened?" Chris asked. "I heard you shouting for Olivia, so we followed you. When we got to the field, everyone was screaming, but you were gone. An ambulance was pulling up."

"Ambulance?" asked Ellie in alarm.

"Dude, I think you broke Olivia's arm," Nicole answered.

"I found Izzy, that new flute player, crying in the band room because Olivia had been making fun of her. I guess I just snapped," Ellie confessed, "I wasn't thinking. I just thought I'd scare her. I lifted her in the air in front of all her friends! Everyone's going to know about our powers now!" Ellie started to sob. She was ashamed she had just exposed their magic secret.

"How bad was it?" Nicole asked Kat.

"I was in the gym when it started," Kat explained, "When I got out to the field, Olivia was hovering ten feet up. There were about fifteen kids close enough to see what was happening. Some of them were recording it on their phones." They all groaned at this news. "It took me a second to figure out how it was happening. Ellie was shouting at her, so I figured she was doing it somehow. I grabbed her before she could lift Olivia any higher and brought her here."

"The whole thing was recorded," Nicole stated flatly. Ellie felt bad enough. Now her friend was mad at her. She sobbed harder.

"Is there any logical explanation we can give?" suggested Chris. They all remained silent.

"It may be time to come clean," answered Kat, "I've been hiding this for three years. It's made my life difficult. Maybe it won't be so bad if people know."

"But what if the witch takes our powers away as punishment?" whined Ellie. She had decided that she never, ever wanted to be that scared, powerless little girl again.

"I'm sorry, the what?" asked Kat.

"The witch that lives in the locker," explained Ellie, rather matter-of-factly, wiping her tears, "She said she can take away our powers."

"She what?" asked Chris and Nicole in unison. Their tones were very different, however. Nicole sounded upset; Chris sounded hopeful.

"The witch told me today that she would take away my power if I didn't hurt Olivia," Ellie admitted.

"There's a witch in the locker that told you to hurt people?" questioned Kat, "I just saw a ball of light. I never heard anything."

"Only Ellie's heard the voice," Chris explained. They were all looking at Ellie. She felt trapped. It was all her fault. She was the evil one. They used their powers to defend themselves. She used hers to harm. The witch knew only Ellie was capable of such villainy. Ellie had made her decision. Now she would have to live with it.

"I'd better get home." Ellie walked away from her friends, if they were still her friends. She went slowly. She didn't want to be there, but she didn't want to be anywhere.

· · · ● · ● · · ·

And so goes Ellie the Evil, walking towards her villain arc. There's no denying fate. It's time to embrace the darkness.

Still, there may be a glimmer of hope for Ellie. After all, this *is* the part of the tale where the hero is supposed go it alone to conquer the evil witch, a metaphor for the evil within. Ellie marries Simon, and the story ends. Nothing ever happens after marriage. You're just stuck in wedded bliss. Forever.

# Chapter 8

# Damage Control

When Ellie reached her house, she was reluctant to enter. She was not ready to face her mother asking how her day had been. It amazed Ellie that something so innocuous as a greeting could become such a dreaded thing. She wasn't a very good liar. Her Mom knew her too well anyway for that. Ellie sat on the porch until her mother texted her.

*Are you okay? The news is reporting a student was injured at your school.*

Ellie decided it was time to go inside. She didn't want her mother to get mad at her too.

"Hey, Mom!" Ellie tried to sound cheerful but failed.

"Ellie! Are you okay? Do you know what happened at school?" Her mother sounded alarmed. The local news was on the television.

"Reports of a hoax gone wrong at Cecilia Payne High School have been pouring in today," announced the reporter. They were showing cellphone footage of Olivia suspended in the air. "It appears some students were shooting a prank video of a girl levitating into the air when the cables broke. She fell to the ground, breaking her arm in the process." Ellie couldn't believe her luck. They thought it was a hoax. Ellie wasn't even visible in the footage.

"Like they said, Mom, some stupid kids were playing a joke. I'm fine," Ellie assured her mother.

"Where's your trombone? You promised to practice this weekend," her mother asked.

Her trombone! Ellie had completely forgotten. *"Well, there's a witch in my locker who tells me to hurt people, and then this girl was crying in the band room, so I dropped my trombone to break a girl's arm. Oh, and I have superpowers, forgot to mention. So, I left my trombone in the band room while I was exacting vengeance."* Nope, not ready to reveal her villainous secret to her parents yet.

"I forgot it," Ellie replied. It wasn't a lie.

"Oh, Ellie. I'm not sure what's going on with you lately. You know you can talk to me, right?" Ellie nodded vaguely. Her mother was clearly disappointed in her. At least she didn't know the real reason Ellie forgot her trombone.

Ellie went up to her room to assess the damage she had caused. Her social media channels were flooded with the news of Olivia Hurley levitating. Ellie found a video posted by Olivia's friend, Jade. Jade caught most of the incident on camera, including Ellie's shouts, but not her face. Ellie scrolled through the comments. They ranged from, "Nice try, but you can see the wires" to "OMG aliens!" Few people outside of those in immediate view of the incident believed it was real.

Okay, Ellie could work with that. She checked her texts last. There was only one. It was from Chris.

*Meet at warehouse @ midnight. Worried about you. XOXO*

· · · · **·** · **·** · · ·

Ellie snuck out of the house and headed to the warehouse. She tried to mentally prepare for the intervention she was certainly about to face from her friends. Every excuse she played out in her head led to the same conclusion: she was wrong. Sure enough, Nicole and Kat were already waiting with Chris. Ellie kept her eyes on the ground.

"Are you okay?" asked Chris, pulling Ellie in for a hug. Ellie nodded tentatively, keeping her eyes on the ground. Then she felt a hug from behind: Nicole. Even Kat joined in. They were still united. Ellie felt a small amount of relief.

"Dude, we were talking after you left. We have to find out who or what this witch is," Nicole explained, "We're not going to let her take you down, even if it means losing our powers. We all agreed." Ellie noticed the other two were nodding.

"But how?" asked Ellie.

"I'm going to break into Dr. Sophia's office," Nicole resolved, "It's a long shot, but it's the only place we can think of to start. There may be something in her files about other students with magic. This probably didn't start with us."

"There's something else," added Chris, "Kat can fuel her power with any emotion, and it's evolved."

Ellie looked hopefully at Kat.

"It's true", Kat acknowledged, "At first, I was teleporting to random locations to escape my bullies. I had no control when I was just fueled by fear. It took a while, but I was finally able to teleport wherever I wanted to go by using all of my emotions together. Last year, I was getting so good at it, I tried teleporting with my sister. It took practice and patience, but I could eventually teleport both of us. Now I can do this!" Kat held her hand up and a plushie appeared out of thin air.

"How?" Ellie gasped.

"Well, I have to know exactly where an object is. I can't move the object exactly, but I can summon it to me by imagining a portal around it. I can teleport to the object without having to physically go there. It's like an in-between space."

Somehow this turned into science class. Ellie tried to picture Kat's in-between space.

"How did you practice?" asked a very curious Chris.

"It's funny. Dr. Sophia taught me these breathing techniques for my anxiety. I thought it was useless at first. But when I tried it, it helped me calm down and tune out distractions. I researched different breathing and meditation exercises and used those principles to harness my power. I started envisioning teleportation as a portal. It gave me something concrete to focus on. I would visualize where I wanted to go, then imagined the portal that would get me there. Now it's second nature."

Chris, Nicole, and Kat chatted excitedly about the newfound possibilities for their powers. It was agreed that Kat would work with

Chris first to help him control the intensity of his senses. Nicole tried to shapeshift into animals but ended up as humans resembling animals. Ellie had renewed enthusiasm as well. But something was different. She felt removed from the other three as they joked and shared stories. Ellie knew she should feel relief that her friends were not mad over the Olivia incident, but she almost wanted them to be upset with her.

Ellie walked home knowing what she had to do. She would check in with Olivia tomorrow. Ellie had no idea what she would say or do. Ellie was afraid that Olivia would convince the world that the incident wasn't a hoax, but she was no longer afraid of Olivia herself. Ellie wasn't sure if she should approach Olivia with threats or kindness. The old Ellie would apologize and beg for mercy. But the old Ellie was gone.

# Chapter 9

# Unlikely Besties

The next morning, Ellie woke dreading what she must do. She played out different scenarios in her head on how her conversation with Olivia might go. Ellie's first thought was to be truthful and apologize.

*"I'm really sorry I got carried away with the power my magic locker gave me. The witch told me to make you pay for your insults and threats. What was I supposed to do?"*

Hmm, maybe Ellie should leave the witch out of it. In fact, if Ellie didn't mention the locker at all, perhaps Olivia would forget Ellie magically lifted her into the air. Yes, that could work.

*"I'm so sorry I yelled at you. You were being an enormous asshole. Oh, you levitated? How did I miss that?"*

Sounds good. Maybe complete denial would be better.

*"I heard you broke your arm. I brought you some muffins!"*

People *have* to like you when you bring them muffins. It's just a fact. But Olivia doesn't deserve muffins. A stronger approach would be better.

*"Bitch, you trifle with my crew again and you'll be levitating on Mars!"* Ellie had never called anyone a bitch before. It felt good to think it; she just wasn't sure she would have the guts to actually say it.

"Ellie, what are you thinking about?" Her mother's voice brought her back to the present. Ellie had poured herself a bowl of cereal on autopilot while debating which tactic to use on Olivia.

"Nothing, Mom. Just some schoolwork I have to take care of today," her sort-of-truth gave her an idea. "Yeah, there's a group project thing. It might take a while." Now Ellie had an excuse to be gone all day.

"Okay. Well, be home by 6 for dinner then," her mother said with a kiss as she left for work.

Ellie got ready slowly, hoping the perfect approach would come to her. She avoided looking in the mirror while doing her hair. The Ellie-in-the-mirror had been far too judgmental lately. She glanced at herself when she finished. Several curls hadn't made it into the ponytail. She took one long, frustrated look at the mirror, then pulled out the ponytail tie. She shook her head and let her curls fly. They landed in a mess all around her face. No matter, she thought. Let them laugh. She was sick of hiding. She grabbed her old lady backpack and headed out the door to face Olivia Hurley.

As Ellie marched to her doom, she noticed the beautiful day mocking her. She pointed her face towards the sunlight, trying to let its warmth comfort her. No, this glorious day wasn't meant for her to enjoy. The walk should have taken fifteen minutes, but Ellie stretched it to an hour. She drew in a deep breath, exhaled out slowly, and gathered her courage. She approached the front door, afraid she may have the wrong house, even more afraid she had the right house.

Suddenly, Ellie heard yelling coming from the back of the house.

"Get here right now, loser!" Ellie wondered who Olivia's victim was as she snuck toward the direction of the yelling. It continued as she crept, "You're always getting me into trouble! I wish you were never born!" Ellie realized they were in the backyard. She stayed hidden, trying to figure out her next move. She heard a slap. Ellie launched around the corner to reveal herself without thinking, prepared to help whoever Olivia's victim was. Ellie froze in her tracks. Olivia was on the ground crying. A much larger, more muscular, equally beautiful, and considerably more terrifying version of Olivia had her hand out to hit Olivia again. Without hesitation, Ellie used her power to swoop up a patio table and used it to shield Olivia. The assailant was momentarily baffled. She gathered herself, pushed the table aside, and continued towards Olivia. Ellie concentrated all her fear on the girl's feet and pulled her back. The girl cursed and struggled to gain control. Ellie held the girl firmly in place but began to panic, having no idea what to do next. She looked at Olivia; Olivia looked back at her. They ran for it. Ellie heard a thud as she released the terrifying not-Olivia. "This way!" shouted Olivia, heading towards the elementary school. Ellie hadn't even realized they had been running in the same direction. Ellie followed Olivia, noticing that the cast on her arm was slowing her down. Ellie looked back. They were not being chased. They slowed down and sat on the swing set.

"So, it *was* you lifting me into the air," said Olivia, "Are you like a witch or something?"

"Or something," Ellie replied. They were silent for a moment. "Was that your sister?"

"Yeah," Olivia answered, then reluctantly added, "Thanks."

Ellie nodded. She wasn't sure if Olivia was going to hug her or hit her. When she did neither, Ellie said what she needed to say, "I'm sorry about your arm. I was just trying to scare you. I didn't mean to hurt you."

Olivia nodded. After another moment's silence, she asked, "Could you not tell the kids at school about this?"

Relief swarmed over Ellie. "As long as you don't tell them I'm a witch."

Olivia smirked. "It's not like anyone would believe me anyway." She got up, looking at Ellie as if she were about to say something else. She shrugged instead and walked away, in the opposite direction of her house.

*"Well, that was nothing like I thought would happen,"* thought Ellie as she remained on her swing. She reflected on what just happened. Would things be different between her and Olivia now? That's how it happened in movies. Olivia would become her unlikely bestie. They would all live happily ever...oh, never mind.

Ellie laughed at the absurdity of it all. She remembered how Tiffany-Ann Trombley had tormented her on that very playground. While the other kids played hopscotch and jumped rope together, Ellie played alone in fear, hoping Tiffany-Ann would leave her be. Even after the day's events with Olivia, Ellie couldn't help fantasizing about getting revenge on Tiffany-Ann. She imagined Little Tiffany-Ann chasing Little Ellie around the swing set. Little Ellie raised the swings at her command, ensnaring Little Tiffany-Ann in their chains. Little Ellie lifted her high in the air while she screamed, then squashed her like a bug. Ellie caught herself smiling a little too deviously at the thought of it.

Ellie wondered what the witch would think. Would she know what happened today with Olivia? She knew about the notorious pencil incident. Chris' power reached for miles at least. Ellie thought the witch's reach must be similar. After all, their powers came from the witch. So why is Ellie the only one who could hear her? Perhaps the witch used telepathy. Then she would know everything Ellie did. Yikes.

A notification buzzed from her phone. It was a text from Nicole.

*Broke into office. Meet at warehouse NOW*

# Chapter 10

## The Missing Girl

Ellie ran to the warehouse faster than she'd ever run before. She found Chris and Kat were already inside. They were sitting cross-legged on the ground, Chris wearing a blindfold.

"I acknowledge Ellie's presence. I now return to my white room," he said.

"Ooooookay," Ellie replied, unsure of what was happening. Their calmness made her even more anxious for Nicole to arrive.

"Shhhh," whispered Kat calmly. Ellie was on pins and needles but allowed them to finish...whatever this was.

"When you are ready, take a moment to connect back to the Earth, then remove your blindfold," Kat instructed. Chris inhaled slowly, held his breath, and removed his blindfold on exhale.

"Namaste. Nicole approaches," he announced in a regal manner. Ellie wondered where his staff and wizard hat were.

"Again, you don't have to say 'namaste'," laughed Kat.

"I know, I just like it," Chris retorted, returning to his usual goofiness, "Ellie! I love your hair!"

Ellie was about to burst with excitement. "Where's Nicole?"

Chris listened a moment. "She stopped at the convenience store. Wait...she's just shifted into an employee. Um, now she's running this way. Why? What's going on?"

"Didn't you get her text?" asked Ellie. The other two shook their heads and reached for their phones.

"We turned them off so Chris could focus on controlling his magic with meditation," explained Kat. They read the message and looked at each other in alarm.

Nicole came running into the warehouse, her arms full of snacks. Ellie was no longer shocked by Nicole's rebelliousness, but Kat rolled her eyes in judgment.

"Hey! Got us some snacks! You guys are never going to believe what I found!" Nicole dropped the snacks and sat. She transformed into Dr. Sophia.

"So, Dr. Sophia's computer doesn't have facial recognition," she told them.

"You went to the school today? How did you get in?" asked Kat. Nicole answered by turning into the school's custodian, holding up his keyring.

"You have keys to the school?" Ellie exclaimed.

"Of course," Nicole replied nonchalantly, "Anyway, I thought that was it. I tried a few passwords but didn't want to chance getting locked out of the computer because then she would know someone had broken in. So I started going through her desk drawers to see if I could find anything. Most had pens, paper, stapler...that sort of thing. But one drawer was locked. Dude, it took me ten minutes to pick that lock. None of the other desks at school have a lock like that," Nicole smiled sneakily at Kat. Kat crossed her arms reproachfully. Nicole continued, "Anyway, I figured something good had to be in there, right? Well, I found THIS!" Nicole proudly held up her phone for the others to see. It was a photo of a manila folder with 'Locker?' written on it. They all gasped.

"There was so much stuff in there. I took as many photos as I could before security could catch me, but I didn't get all of it." Nicole rapidly scrolled through the photos to show the others. She stopped on one of a news clipping. "This is an old article about a girl who went missing. Listen to this: 'Local girl Eliza Fritz is still missing under mysterious circumstances. Fritz was reported missing when she failed to return home from Andrew Johnson High School two weeks ago. Rumors of unexplained light phenomena and UFOs have plagued the investigation, making the case difficult for police to confirm any leads. Fritz's parents have issued a reward for tips regarding their daughter's whereabouts. Please contact the police department with any information.' Then there's a phone number," Nicole concluded, looking up at the others.

"Where's Andrew Johnson High?" asked Chris.

"It's our high school," answered Kat, "They renamed it in the nineties."

"The nineties?" exclaimed Ellie, "Nicole, does that article have a date on it?"

"Um, yeah," replied Nicole, looking at her phone, "May 25th, 1984."

"1984? Do you think the magic locker has been around that long?" questioned Ellie. Nicole started transforming rapidly.

"Either she was abducted by aliens, or the witch took her," concluded Chris, looking at Ellie, "Do you think she's still missing?" They all pulled out their phones to search the name. Ellie's search brought up several people named Eliza Fritz, but none in their area. She scrolled until she found an old website on cold case files.

"They never found her," said Chris solemnly. Ellie was deflated. Eliza Fritz could have been the one person who knew about the witch.

"What else was in the folder?" Kat asked Nicole.

"I didn't have much time to read any of it. Here, I'll send you the files," Nicole answered, transforming back into herself.

"I think we need to be careful. Maybe the witch gave us these powers to feed off our energy. If she had something to do with Eliza Fritz's disappearance, we may all be in danger, but most of all Ellie," Kat chose the last words carefully. Ellie realized they were all looking at her again. Kat gently put her hands on Ellie's shoulders. "Ellie, I want you to let me know if you need help. I can get you at a moment's notice and take you somewhere safe," her words were comforting. Kat's soothing tone reminded Ellie of Dr. Sophia. Dr. Sophia!

"Wait!" exclaimed Ellie, "This means Dr. Sophia knows about the locker!"

Chris was viewing the photos Nicole had sent. "I don't know how much, though. It looks like she's been researching strange events and troubled students. Since most of the notes are hand-written, I think she's keeping some student information out of the school's official records."

"Should we tell Dr. Sophia about us?" asked Ellie.

"I don't know," replied Kat. "I want to read through everything Nicole got first. What if Dr. Sophia wants to use the locker's power for the wrong reasons? Maybe she's trying to find magic users for experiments? I mean, haven't you ever wondered what someone with a doctorate is doing as a school counselor in our microscopic town?"

Ellie had not. She had wondered how a woman who looked like an international spy ended up there, though.

"I don't think Dr. Sophia is evil," asserted Ellie.

"That could just be her psychiatric tricks!" proposed Nicole, turning into a comically villainous version of the doctor.

"I agree with Kat," said Chris, "I think we should wait until we know more. Let's digest this information first."

The four sat down and began to read the information in silence. Dr. Sophia was careful not to include any identifying information in her notes. While Ellie appreciated the confidentiality, it made it impossible to figure out when the notes were taken, or who may also have magic powers.

"Look at the tenth photo," Kat directed. Ellie found the photo. It showed a partially torn typed letter with '1984' hand-written on the top right corner. "Someone was expelled, but their details are missing."

The alarm on Ellie's phone chimed to the tune of Sunshine. "I have to get home for dinner!" she exclaimed.

"Me too," said Kat, "See you tomorrow?" They agreed to meet at the warehouse again. Ellie walked home, head buzzing with thoughts of Eliza Fritz.

# Chapter 11

# The Black Cat

"What's wrong? You've barely touched your pork chop," asked Ellie's mother during dinner, "It's your favorite!"

Actually, Ellie hated pork chops and meat in general. Seeing the bones was too much for her.

"Sorry, Mom. Just thinking about that school project."

"What is it on?" her father asked, "Maybe we can help."

"Nah, I've got it. Just some stuff about space." Her parents eyed her suspiciously. Why was she such a bad liar?

"Well, okay. Just let us know if you need anything." Ellie was relieved her father dropped it. She wanted to tell her parents about everything that was happening but was worried about their reaction. They had both been working so hard lately. She didn't want to pile anything else on. Or maybe Ellie just wanted to continue using her power unchecked. Surely her parents would punish her for what she's done. Ellie pushed that thought out of her mind.

Ellie did think of one thing they may be able to help her with, however. "Do either of you know a family named Fritz from around here?"

"You mean the girl who went missing?" replied her mother, "So sad. Her mother died of a broken heart soon after, or so the story goes. Why do you ask?"

"Oh, there's a kid in school whose last name is Fritz. Just wondering," Wow. Why was lying so difficult?

"Well, it's probably not the same family," Ellie's mother answered, "The father left town, and I've not heard of another family with that name." Ellie's father shrugged to indicate he hadn't either.

After dinner, Ellie retreated to her room. She put on her headphones and danced around unencumbered to MSC. She imagined Simon dancing with her, enjoying a pretend concert together. Her mobile danced and played with her. She sat on her bed, fully content with the fantasy. But wait, how was the mobile moving? Ellie studied its movements, now slowing to a stop. The fan was off; the windows closed. She got up and waved her hand around the mobile, checking for a breeze. The planets danced around her fingers. Ellie smiled in amusement. Her phone pinged. It was a notification from MSC's social media. It was a photo of a mobile of the solar system, similar to Ellie's.

· · · · • · • · · ·

Ellie never liked Sundays. Sunday waits for something that never comes. It is a day of longing for Saturday and dreading Monday. Ellie wanted to skip this particular Sunday most of all. There was no telling what Monday would be like at school in the wake of the Olivia Incident. Ellie held out hope that everyone would just forget the levitating student. Stranger things have happened.

Ellie got to the warehouse early. She sat on the floor, leaned against the decaying wall, and waited for her friends. She peered out of a broken window at the grey sky before pulling out her phone. The first thing she checked was MSC's social media accounts. Nope, she didn't imagine it. The last post was a mobile of the solar system. She scrolled through the other clues. The band's followers had figured out many of them as the weeks passed. As it happened, Holst didn't just compose the March they were playing in band. He also composed something called 'The Planets' as well. Ellie's apologies owed to Holst were mounting. There were still arguments about the computer keyboard. Some fans thought the clue was a pun on the space bar, others expected a new keyboardist to be announced. Ellie wondered when the album would be released. What was the band waiting for? Waiting. Ellie's patience was running thin these days. She felt like she was always waiting for something.

Ellie decided to scroll through the photos Nicole sent again. It seemed everything was a clue she could not decipher. The answer must be in there somewhere. Was the witch truly a danger to Ellie and her friends? What really happened to Eliza Fritz? Ellie called the phone number at the bottom of the news article. Of course, it was disconnected.

Ellie heard a noise coming from the far corner of the warehouse. With a quick blow of the wind and rustling of leaves, a black cat with bright green eyes emerged from the darkness. It walked towards Ellie, stopping several feet from her. They stared at each other. Ellie got up to pet it, but it ran away. Ellie wanted to follow it, but her friends showed up at that moment in the corner from which that cat emerged. They were holding hands and laughing.

"Ellie! There you are!" exclaimed Chris, "Kat just teleported us around! It was intense!" The three were positively giddy. Ellie felt a pang of jealousy.

"It was incredible!" added Nicole. Pang, pang.

"Hey, are you okay?" asked Chris, sensing Ellie's disappointment.

"Yeah, sure. Kat got both of you?" Ellie tried to ask nonchalantly.

"Well, we tried to get you, but you had already left," explained Kat, "But listen, I could teleport to your house even though I'd never been there using Chris as a guide. Do you know what this means? I can go to Paris with someone who's been there!" As they all chatted excitedly, Ellie began to let go of her jealousy. They did try to include her, after all. And Paris did sound nice.

"I don't mean to brag, but I ate breakfast this morning without gagging!" proclaimed Chris. "The meditation is working! I'm so much more focused now!" Ellie was truly happy for her friend. She felt guilty for enjoying her magic power while Chris had to struggle.

"Kat, can you guide me? I want to be able to transform into animals!" asked Nicole, "I really want to be a ferocious, man-eating tiger!" Nicole attempted to become a tiger but looked more like a cross between Mr. Joshi and Dr. Sophia.

"Um, maybe you should start smaller," suggested Kat.

"What about a cat?" suggested Ellie, thinking of her new friend, the black cat.

"Boring!" quipped Nicole as they all sat down.

"Okay, everyone close your eyes and relax. Take a few deep breaths and try to clear your mind," instructed Kat. Ellie attempted to clear her mind, but her brain was a swarm of activity. "Breathe in, breathe out, breathe in, breathe out," Kat chanted slowly. Ellie had to admit Kat's voice was very soothing. "Picture a sunny day. You're lying in a field. A warm breeze envelops you as you connect to the Earth." Ellie snuck a peek at the others. Even Nicole was taking it seriously. Okay, Ellie, you just have to try.

Kat guided them through a relaxation exercise, starting by focusing on their toes and ending at the top of their heads. Ellie definitely felt more relaxed, but anxiety and doubt still plagued her.

"Remain still and connected to the Earth," continued Kat, "Nicole, I want you to picture yourself as a cat. Imagine every detail of what you want your cat to look like. Once you have complete focus of what you will become, reach deep down into your magic to create the space you need to transform." They remained silent for a moment. Ellie felt herself drifting off. It was like the dizziness she felt when her power first emerged, but more comforting. Maybe it was that she understood it more now, or because she was surrounded by her friends. Ellie imagined her own power lurking deep inside of her. A new place opened in her mind: a vision of space and magic. It seemed familiar, like something that had always been waiting, ready to emerge. She imagined balls of light dancing around her.

Ellie woke to a scream. Nicole had black cat ears and whiskers. The rest of her appearance remained human. It was not cute. They all started laughing and shrieking with delight. Nicole looked at herself on her phone.

"I am so ugly!" she laughed as she examined herself.

"I think it's an improvement," joked Ellie. She immediately regretted the comment, afraid it may have upset her friend. Thankfully Nicole just rolled her eyes and giggled. With a scrunch of her face, Nicole transformed into Ellie, then back to herself, sans ears and whiskers.

"Ew. I do not like that," Ellie said with a disgusted look on her face. "Seeing yourself is really bizarre."

"Agreed," added Chris and Kat in unison. Nicole shrugged.

"Well, we established that you can transform into animals," concluded Kat, "You just need to keep practicing."

"Man-eating tiger, here I come!" exclaimed Nicole as she grabbed Ellie and spun her around. Nicole let go as Ellie continued her spin. The spin made her dizzy but elated. She came to a halt and noticed her friends staring at her in shock.

"What's wrong?" Ellie asked, panicking.

"Dude, look!" Nicole handed her phone to Ellie. Ellie took it to look at herself. Nicole was on the screen. Ellie switched the camera mode to face front. Still Nicole. Confused, Ellie frantically swapped modes. Slowly, selfie-mode Nicole faded back into Ellie's image. Ellie looked at Nicole in amazement.

"Did you just transform me into you?" questioned Ellie. The words sounded ridiculous.

"I think so maybe," responded Nicole, "I have no idea how that just happened." Nicole started jumping around in excitement. "I just turned Ellie into me! I can create my own army of man-eating-Nicole-tigers!"

· · · ● · ● · ● · · ·

Yes, dance and laugh, Ellie. Remain oblivious to the path you must travel. You don't think that witch will remain in the locker forever, do you?

# Chapter 12

# A Swirling Darkness

That night, Ellie sat on her bed watching her mobile.

"What do you have to do with it?" she interrogated. It dangled from the ceiling, motionless. Ellie wondered what her life had come to, talking to ceiling accoutrements and expecting answers. She narrowed her eyes in scrutiny. "I'm watching you!" The mobile just hung there, helpless.

Ellie allowed her brain to plan her wedding to Simon before reviewing the day's events. Mind uncluttered by romance, she tried to recall the vision she had during Kat's meditation. She kept an eye on the mobile, just in case. She remembered darkness that wasn't entirely black. Lights like stars were scattered about, some bright as Sirius, others just a vague hint of something that once was. It was like she saw beyond the solar system; it was as familiar as it was unfamiliar. She wondered if this was what Kat's in-between space was like.

Ellie took off her glasses and put them on the nightstand. The mobile became nothing but a blur without them. She closed her eyes: "Inhale in, exhale out." She remembered Kat's words best she could and began to envision the world beyond worlds again. The black cat crept into her vision. "Shoo!" she ordered. The cat simply stared at her in response. It turned from her and walked towards the forming vision. The picture in Ellie's mind was clearer now. She followed the cat. A path of light formed just in front of them. Many other paths were forking in all directions, but the cat seemed to know where it was headed. Ellie discovered she was more curious about the other paths than the one they were taking. Balls of light bounced around her. Some investigated the travelers; others didn't react to them at all. Ellie and the cat walked silently, the path forming as they went. Ellie wondered if the cat was creating the path or simply following it. The path stayed straight; the space around them moved left or right as they went instead, like a compass needle. Finally, Ellie saw a shape forming out of starlight in front of them. The locker! It remained shut until Ellie approached it. Suddenly the locker burst open, sucking Ellie inside.

Ellie woke with a gasp. She was startled to see it was morning. How long had she been in the world beyond worlds? Was it just a dream? Was it an invitation or a warning?

She got out of bed to get ready for an uncertain Monday. She tried doing something with her curls, adamant about stopping with the ponytails. It was time to show the school the real Eleanor McNeil: a Pluto-loving, trombone-playing, old-backpack-wearing, purple-obsessed, curly-haired wielder of magic.

To her surprise, Kat, Chris, and Nicole were waiting for Ellie outside of her house. They were making polite conversation with her mother.

"It's about time I met your friends!" her mother said cheerfully, "And they're so delightful! Oh, I'm so glad you left your hair down today! I always loved your curls! You kids have a great day at school! Love you, honey!" Ellie's mother gave Ellie their traditional kiss on the head.

"How embarrassing!" Ellie muttered to her friends.

"I wish I had that," Chris lamented. It occurred to Ellie that Chris never mentioned his parents, only his brother. It was hard for her to imagine a life without the support of her parents. Perhaps she took them for granted.

They chatted nervously as they walked towards Cecilia Payne High School. None of them knew quite what to expect. No matter what happened, they would remain a united front. The reactions were mixed as they approached the school's entrance. Some kids avoided them, others ignored them, one group chided them, but to Ellie's surprise, most applauded them. It felt like a slow-motion scene in a movie. She was the hero, not the villain. High-fives all around!

"Do you think they know we all have magic powers?" whispered Nicole.

"Maybe. Someone could have seen me teleport," suggested Kat. Ellie noticed Simon heading towards them. He nodded to Chris then looked straight into Ellie's eyes. His deep, dark brown eyes entranced her.

"I hear you caused quite a commotion on Friday." His voice seeped into Ellie's brain. "Yeah" was all she managed to utter as he continued walking down the hallway. Chris and Ellie sank into each other with a sigh.

"Well, that's disgusting," joked Nicole. Ellie flushed with embarrassment.

"I think you're going to be okay," Kat said to Ellie, observing the other students, "Well, then, I guess I'll see you guys later!" The friends parted ways. Ellie proceeded to her locker. It opened to a sight Ellie hadn't seen...or noticed...before. Beyond the ball of light was a deepening, swirling darkness. She reached towards it, but her hand hit the back of the locker. She studied it for a bit before heading to class.

When Ellie entered the math room, Olivia darted her gaze toward the ground. The other students watched silently as Ellie took her seat. Ellie wished she had a knife to cut the tension. Even Mrs. Canter seemed to be waiting for a fight to break out between her and Olivia. *"Sorry to disappoint,"* thought Ellie, *"That bridge has already been crossed."* Mrs. Canter started class after what felt like an eternity but was more like thirty seconds. Ellie sunk into her seat, exhaling out all the anxiety she was feeling. It was going to be okay.

· · ● · ● · ● · ·

You're not really going to believe that, are you?

· · ● · ● · ● · ·

During band, Ellie decided to investigate her locker again in privacy. She apologized to Holst and once again excused herself for a bathroom break. Nicole watched her go with a quizzical look on her face. Ellie shrugged in response and took off towards the locker.

"Hello, Ms. Witch?" Ellie felt more than a little silly with her head inside her locker. Sometimes you do what you must.

"Mmmmmmmmmm," oozed the witch in response. Ellie hoped for a little more than that.

"Were you in my dream last night?"

"Ahhhhhhh, what is a dream other than moments of your waking life?" Oh, goody, more mysterious babble.

"Why am I the only one who can hear you?" The question came out more demanding than Ellie had planned, but she was starting to get frustrated. There was a long pause before Ellie received her answer:

"Because only you can free me," the witch's voice had lost some of its edge with her reply. Her signature creepiness was still there, but the desperation was obvious.

"How can I free you?" Ellie asked in alarm. It had never occurred to her that the witch was somehow trapped.

"Embrace your power." That again. Ellie took a moment to form her next question but was interrupted by Chris running towards her.

"Was that the witch?" he practically shouted.

"Wait...you heard that?" asked Ellie in surprise.

"She asked you to free her and told you to embrace your power!" Chris sounded genuinely excited.

"I'm not the only one who can hear her?" Ellie should have felt relief. Instead, she was a bit disappointed.

"No! It's okay. Ellie, you're not alone. I realized the other day that I could hear more than I knew. By blocking out taste and smell, my hearing and sight are now more controllable than ever! I must not have heard the witch because I was hearing too many other noises!" Chris hugged Ellie in a comforting embrace.

· · · · ● · ● · · · ·

No, Ellie, you're not alone. Or are you? The hero must walk alone, or so the tales say. One by one, the gallant knights fall to the dragon until the unlikely underdog remains. Dragon gets slayed; the distressed damsel is saved. Still, her friends are being rather persistent in their support. Maybe we can fix that.

# Chapter 13: The Unluckiest of Chapters

"You can't do it, Ellie," demanded Kat, "Not until we know what happened to Eliza Fritz. The witch may be targeting you to take next."

"It doesn't matter. I don't even know how to go about freeing her anyway," Ellie was feeling defensive. She pretended to look around the warehouse to deflect her emotions. What was once between her and the witch was now everyone's concern, so it seemed. Why were her friends so prejudiced against witches anyway? Ellie wondered if they weren't just jealous that the witch chose her instead of them. She was still a bit deflated that Chris could hear the witch too. She hadn't realized how special it made her feel, like she had purpose. Ellie's eyes paused at the corner where she first saw the cat, but it did not come to defend her.

"Look, why don't we try to meditate together again? Maybe we can open the in-between space and try to get some answers. At least it can help me and Nicole if we can experience it too," suggested Chris. Ellie nodded in agreement, determined not to let her negativity ruin her friendships.

They sat in their usual arrangement and began to breathe slowly and rhythmically. Ellie tried to calm herself, but her center was a big, wobbly mess that refused to connect to the Earth. Her brain wouldn't clear itself as thought after thought crept in unfiltered. First up was Simon, gazing into her eyes. *"Nope, not right now,"* she told herself. Next, she wondered when Dr. Sophia would have an open appointment. Her schedule was booked solid as of late. Something about levitating students affected some people more than others. Then there was the mobile, Mars, and the entire My Sister Cellophane situation. Ellie smiled slightly as the band's members Miles, Graham, Sarah, and Terrance appeared in her clouded brain. Try as she might, she couldn't push them aside. They stared at her intently. Miles' mouth was moving, but Ellie could not hear the words.

"What are you trying to tell us?" asked Chris. The vision faded away with a flash of forked light. A discerning breeze circled around them.

"You saw them too?" Ellie exclaimed, "You saw MSC?"

"Yes!" everyone exclaimed.

"What was Miles saying?" Ellie asked Chris.

"I don't know! I couldn't hear him," Chris answered, "Was that really them? But how?"

"Ohhhhhh guys, we are connected to rock stars!" Nicole transformed into each of MSC's members. "Do you think we can contact Taxidermy Dragon next?" She looked absolutely serious.

"I think we all went to the in-between space together!" Kat was elated. They chatted excitedly for a moment until Kat announced, "Oh crap! I'm late for dinner!" With a nod goodbye, Kat vanished.

Ellie checked her phone for the time. She, too, was late. She said her goodbyes and headed home, excited about the possibilities of exploring the in-between space.

· · · ● · ● · · ·

After dinner, Ellie went to her room and once again stared at the mobile. She recalled the day's events. Why did she feel such jealousy toward her friends? One minute she felt secure, the next: isolated. It occurred to her that she felt the same way with the witch. Sometimes Ellie was afraid of the witch, but mostly, Ellie felt empowered by her. Ellie knew she should be cautious; however, she couldn't escape the idea that she, alone, would save the day.

An online search revealed nothing as to the whereabouts of Eliza Fritz's father. Ellie studied the photos Nicole took in Dr. Sophia's office. If only Ellie could talk with Dr. Sophia! Maybe the doctor would confide in Ellie all she knew about the locker, the witch, and Eliza Fritz. Although the names were redacted, Ellie could draw a few conclusions from the files: most of the kids had unstable home lives, they all attended her high school (some when it was Andrew Johnson High), and the dates ranged over several decades. Dr. Sophia had been conducting intense research, so it seemed. Ellie wondered how long Dr. Sophia had been employed at Cecilia Payne High.

A few nagging thoughts crept into Ellie's brain. Ellie had a great home life. It's true that not all the students in Dr. Sophia's research had unstable home lives, but the majority did. Another thing bothering Ellie was the lack of details about Eliza's disappearance. Ellie lost count of the times she searched Eliza's name on the internet. "Rumors of unexplained light phenomena and UFOs" was the best description of the events she could find. Ellie wondered if the witch trapped Eliza inside the in-between space, or if she was trying to get Eliza out. Maybe the witch has nothing to do with Eliza. Eliza may be missing or dead under any circumstances, really. Ellie pictured Eliza Fritz on another planet, enjoying a plentiful life.

What bothered Ellie the most was her unexplained connection to Eliza. Their names were undeniably similar, for one. Eliza's photo on the missing person's page looked a bit like Ellie, too, minus the curls. All of that aside, Ellie thought she could feel Eliza's presence. Ellie knew in her bones that Eliza Fritz was still alive, out there somewhere.

Ellie closed her eyes and pictured the in-between space. Breathing in, and exhaling out, she relaxed her mind and body. She reached out to Eliza Fritz. A wind circled around the room as Ellie entered the in-between space. She was more focused than ever, concentrating on a single purpose. The black cat appeared before her.

"Well, hello," Ellie greeted, "Where were you earlier?" The cat passively glanced in her direction before heading down the path. Ellie followed, often pausing to observe her surroundings. She realized that each forked path had something unique about it. One path appeared brighter as it sprawled out in the distance. Another smelled of burning embers. Ellie instinctively knew to avoid that path. Some of the paths had vague human-like figures, others revealed unfamiliar forms. One path in particular called to Ellie. She stopped at its fork. The longer she stood observing it, the clearer the path became. The lights danced for her invitingly. Ellie noticed the cat was no longer with her. She took one step onto the new path. A swirl of purple light engulfed her. A rush of wind blew her towards a figure taking shape in the distance. The wind landed Ellie next to the figure, now in full form. A girl was huddled over, crying. The image sparked Ellie's memories of Izzy and Olivia. Ellie knew she must help this girl. The girl stopped crying, suddenly aware of Ellie's presence. She slowly turned her head towards Ellie with a slow and unnatural movement. The girl's oversized eyes reflected the starlight around them far too brightly. Her face was distorted and blurry, yet Ellie recognized her immediately: it was Eliza Fritz. Eliza's mouth started to move frantically, but Ellie could not hear the words. In a panic, Ellie gathered all her pain, anger, jealousy, and fear and somehow manifested it into a protective ball of red and black swirling light. Eliza's words became clearer as the ball of light grew brighter.

"Help me, Ellie," Eliza pleaded. The words repeated as if on a recording. Ellie reached out for Eliza, but her hand went right through her, as if Eliza were some sort of projection. Ellie grasped for something tangible, but every attempt caused Eliza's image to ripple. The ball of light grew brighter with Ellie's desperation.

"How? Eliza, how do I help you?" she screamed.

"Embrace your power." The witch's voice echoed for miles. Starlight formed into the shape of the locker. Ellie's ball of light shattered, knocking her to the ground. Momentarily stunned, Ellie started to gather her faculties. She looked around to survey her surroundings. She was in the abandoned warehouse.

# Chapter 14

# Damsel In Distress

Ellie had materialized in the corner of the warehouse where she first saw the cat. She reached for her phone, but realized it was at home on her nightstand with her glasses. Alone and sightless, she started to cry. Her tears were more of frustration than anything. She could walk home without her glasses, but it would be difficult. She could tell from the darkness that it was still nighttime. She started to cry harder as she wished the cat would come to lead her home.

She heard a whooshing sound and her friends running toward her. At first, she thought she had imagined it, still feeling disoriented from being in the other world. Ellie felt them huddle around her in a warm and comforting embrace. She continued to sob for several more minutes before she could gather herself.

Ellie described the incident in the in-between space with as much detail as possible. Her friends listened solemnly.

"I went in tonight, too," said Chris, "I was trying to find Miles to figure out what he was saying. There was music coming from some of the paths. Most of it sounded ancient. So I tried singing "Sunshine" to see if it would draw them out. I went down several paths. Most of them just ended. One led to a huge cave full of treasures like jewelry, mirrors, clocks, and coins."

"Did you take any of it?" interrupted Nicole enthusiastically.

"No, it kept slipping through my hands. It was really weird!" he answered, "So I continued checking paths and ended up in a forest. Glowing red eyes were peeking out from a treetop. It was so creepy! I tried to double back, but the forest formed around me in every direction. I started to panic, and a black cat appeared. That's when I heard Ellie crying. Then I was back in my bed. Luckily Kat woke up when I called her so we could come to get you."

"Black cat?" Ellie exclaimed, "It must be the same one!"

"Look, we should get back home before any of our parents discover we're gone," Kat suggested, "I don't think any of us should travel the in-between space alone right now. It sounds really dangerous. We'll try to help Eliza Fritz, but we go together." Kat was always so practical.

"Aw, no treasure?" whined Nicole, transforming into a queen dripping with jewels.

"Not right now," laughed Kat. One by one, she teleported them back to their homes, saving Ellie for last.

"Please be safe," Kat begged, "I know you want to help Eliza. We all do. But we're meddling in things we know little about." She gave Ellie a hug and vanished.

Ellie laid down on her bed, snuggling into the covers for comfort. She was confused about a great many things. There was one thing she knew for certain, however: Eliza Fritz was trapped, and the locker held the key to her freedom.

· · · · ● · ● · ● · · ·

Over the next few weeks, the four friends walked to the abandoned warehouse after school and traveled the in-between space together. At first, their exploring went nowhere, as they were all being pulled towards different paths. They discovered that focusing on a singular goal before going in helped the navigation go more smoothly. Ellie was anxious to get back to Eliza Fritz, but Kat insisted they learn more about the in-between space first for safety. Ellie knew in her mind that Kat was right, but her heart held a ticking time bomb of urgency to free Eliza.

They were able to find MSC again. However, Miles' words remained silent. Sometimes the band seemed close enough to touch, then disappeared when Ellie reached out for them. The four also tried to summon the cat. It clearly had a mind of its own, popping in and out of view as they traveled. Most of their ventures were reconnaissance missions to try to map the in-between. The more they tried, the more they realized it wasn't possible. The paths constantly changed and shifted. They often argued about which path to follow, but always remained together regardless. They discovered dimly-kit caves, libraries full of books in old languages, mountains made of glowing crystals, and open fields with strange, wandering creatures. One time, a man wearing an oddly shaped, multi-colored suit crossed their path, playing a tune on a flute that was strangely reminiscent of "Sunshine". Ellie giggled and started to follow him mindlessly until Nicole pulled her back. Kat emerged as the natural leader of the group, Chris proved excellent at navigation, Nicole fearlessly rescued them in times of danger, and Ellie kept a journal of notes and drawings from their trips for reference.

The four settled into roles at school, too. Nicole transformed throughout the day to tail Dr. Sophia undetected. Chris watched and listened for anything suspicious. Kat poured through all the clues they had gathered. And Ellie? Well, Ellie made sure no one was being bullied anymore.

When Ellie finally got in to see Dr. Sophia, they both acted like nothing had happened. Ellie was eager to speak with Dr. Sophia about the locker but had promised her friends she wouldn't. The anticipation was agony. Ellie still had a difficult time trusting other people. If anyone deserved her loyalty, it was Kat, Chris, and Nicole. Ellie did wonder why Dr. Sophia didn't bring up the Olivia Incident at all. It was a bit suspicious.

Dr. Sophia did help Ellie with some of her underlying issues. Ellie had not realized how negative her inner thoughts could be at times. Dr. Sophia gave Ellie the task of saying one good thing about herself every morning. Some mornings were easier than others. Sometimes Ellie simply repeated the same good thing from the previous day. But the exercise helped Ellie become more cognizant of the impact of her own thoughts.

As for the witch in the locker, well, she was being quite elusive. Ellie rarely got more than "Embrace your power" from her. It sounded more like a recording now, not unlike the figure of Eliza Fritz asking for help, or Miles' unheard message. Ellie became obsessed with the phrase. "Embrace your power." Hadn't she done that already? Every instinct screamed at Ellie to be cautious, but her curiosity was starting to get the better of her. The darkness in the locker deepened to where Ellie could no longer discern where the back wall truly was. Ellie was still unable to break through, though. She tried to imagine the in-between space, but her hand hit the unseen back of the locker every time.

One night Ellie sat at her desk, looking out of her bedroom window. She watched the snow fall, the first snow of the year. She never imagined having magic powers would grow monotonous. The more established their routine became, the more agitated Ellie got with it. Their research was going nowhere. Meanwhile, Eliza Fritz needed their help. Ellie held her hand up to the cold glass of her window. She found some pleasure in causing the snowflakes to rearrange into different shapes: a castle, a mermaid, a dragon. She laughed as she wondered if mermaids and dragons actually existed.

· · · ● · ● · · ·

Yes, Eleanor McNeil, they exist, just not as you think. There are entire worlds yet to be discovered, as perilous as they are fantastic. They creep into your dreams and haunt your nightmares. But the true monsters live in your world.

# Chapter 15

# A Cosmic Kaleidoscope

There was an air of jubilance throughout the school on the last day before winter break. Students filled the hallways chatting excitedly about their vacation plans. Bullying had ceased almost completely. Ellie could feel the energy pulsating through her. She unleashed her new swagger walk, having practiced at home. She beamed at Simon as he passed. There were paper snowflakes dangling from the hallway's ceiling. Ellie's confidence was growing. With a quick channeling from the in-between space, she caused the snowflakes to swirl around her, one at a time, as she strutted down humming "Sunshine".

Her smile was radiant as she reached her locker. She hummed the final notes of "Sunshine" to greet Nicole, Chris, and Kat, who were waiting there for her.

"Um, isn't that a bit risky?" asked Kat, pointing to the last of the swirling snowflakes. Ellie noticed some of the other students smiling at her.

"Aw, let the girl have her fun!" exclaimed Nicole, putting her arm around Ellie. She scrunched up her face, transforming into an absurdly stern version of a Kat then back to herself again.

"I thought we agreed you wouldn't do that anymore," groaned Kat.

"I can't help it, you're just so pretty!" Nicole laughed, fluttering her eyes.

"It's so weird looking at yourself like that," explained Kat, for the hundredth time.

"Ah, I'm sorry," apologized Nicole, "I'd say I won't do it again, but we all know that's a lie."

Even Kat had to laugh at that.

"Good morning, students," boomed Principal Martinez' voice over the loudspeaker, "I know everyone is excited for winter break. I hope you can all sideline those thoughts and keep your eye on the academic ball today."

Nicole chortled and Kat rolled her eyes. Ellie pulled out her journal.

"Hey! So, I really think we should try to help Eliza now," suggested Ellie rather abruptly, flipping through her notes and sketches. The others awkwardly looked at each other. "Come on, we've been traveling the in-between for weeks now. We're not learning anything new."

"Exactly!" exclaimed Kat, "We're not. That's why I'm hesitant."

The bell rang. Ellie looked hopefully at Chris and Nicole.

"Dude, we'll talk about it later," Nicole assured with a wink before heading to class.

Chris took Ellie by the hand. "Ellie, I'm really worried about this. I want to make sure we're as safe as possible." Ellie let go of Chris' hand in frustration. She slammed her journal shut, turned on her heel and headed to class.

By band time, most of Ellie's joy had returned. She still had an underlying desperation to save Eliza Fritz, however. She felt a persistent, invisible tug pulling her toward the in-between space. But that gave her no right to take it out on Chris. Try as she might to silence it, the voice inside her head kept telling her she wasn't worthy of friends. With a quick mental push to stifle that thought, she forced her inner voice to say one good thing about herself. *"Okay...I'm funny. At times. Maybe only I think so."* It was a start. She texted Chris an apology. She grabbed her trombone, took her seat, nodded to Paul, and turned to Nicole.

"Hello gorgeous!" Nicole greeted, banging on the timpani. Ellie allowed a small amount of fear bubble to the surface and channeled it into the drumstick to the rhythm of "Sunshine". Nicole chortled as she struggled to gain control. Paul rolled his eyes. Ellie had given up on concealing her power from him weeks ago.

After band, Ellie headed to her locker to retrieve her science book. The locker popped open in its usual greeting. The back of the locker swirled like a cosmic kaleidoscope. Ellie was never able to reach through it but tried anyway. Her hand hit the back of the locker.

"Embrace your power," oozed the witch's voice. Ellie's patience was wearing thin. In a flash of frustration, she conjured up a small ball of light and flung it towards the back of the locker. The light dissipated, swirling into the cosmos.

"It is time." The witch's voice echoed out. The voice sounded creepy but assuring. Ellie felt conflicted. She watched the swirling cosmos of the world beyond worlds shift inside the locker. Ellie was entranced.

"It is time," Ellie conceded. She instinctively leaned further into her locker. The hallway faded as Ellie was drawn towards the in-between space. She closed her eyes, inhaled in, exhaled out, and allowed it to take her.

"What are you doing?" yelled Nicole, pulling Ellie out by the arm. Ellie noticed the other students staring at them. "Move on! Nothing to see here!" Nicole shouted at them. She turned to Ellie and whispered, "I thought we were going to discuss this!"

"We have been discussing it!" Ellie whispered back furiously. She reached her hand back into the locker, but it hit the back. "Great! I finally got through the barrier and now it's sealed again." She didn't mean to be angry with Nicole, but her inexplicable need to go through the locker was paramount. Ellie noticed Chris and Kat approaching them.

"We agreed to do this together!" Nicole retorted. Ellie could tell her friend was getting upset. Nicole's face was starting to blur as she tried to prevent herself from shapeshifting.

"Why are you mad at me?" Ellie demanded. Their argument was starting to get louder again. Chris and Kat stood by helplessly, trying to shield others from hearing the conversation.

"Why don't you trust me? I've been nothing but a friend to you!"

Ellie choked back tears of utter frustration as she attempted to conjure up a comeback. She noticed Dr. Sophia marching towards them. The doctor gently placed her hands on Ellie and Nicole's wrists. Ellie's vision flickered as strange thoughts entered her brain, flashing in and out. She couldn't seem to focus. It was like passing hundreds of signs on a highway but not being able to read any of them. She saw glimpses of the locker, the band room, Nicole's basement, and the convenience store She saw herself appear in the distance. A warm, calming rush of love washed over her. Ellie had never seen herself that way before. Tears poured down her face as she realized they were not her thoughts at all: they were Nicole's. The thoughts left Ellie's brain as Dr. Sophia let go. Ellie looked at Nicole, completely speechless.

"Ellie, I had no idea!" Nicole cried, hugging Ellie tightly. They held onto each other for several minutes. When they let go, Dr. Sophia was gone.

"Um, would either of you like to explain what just happened?" asked Chris.

Ellie laughed through her tears. Nicole tried to explain best she could.

"It's like I was in Ellie's brain! I could feel her frustration and suddenly I understood why she was so upset!" Ellie nodded in agreement.

"Dr. Sophia connected you somehow," said Kat.

Ellie stopped crying. "Dr. Sophia has powers?" Ellie wasn't sure why the possibility hadn't occurred to her before. What also occurred to her was the lack of people in the hallway. The bell must have rung at some point during their argument. The four formed an unspoken agreement and swiftly headed to Dr. Sophia's office.

# Chapter 16

# Metaphysical Trickery

D r. Sophia was in her office waiting for them. She had four chairs positioned around her desk. Her laptop was closed. Ellie took a moment to appreciate how good Dr. Sophia looked in her burgundy crushed velvet pantsuit before taking a seat. The doctor opened her mouth to start, but all four started asking questions at once. Dr. Sophia stifled a laugh as she held up her hands to stop them.

"Okay, I understand you have questions, but I must ask you one first: what can you do that other people cannot?" Ellie thought this was a strange question until she realized none of them had actually revealed their powers to Dr. Sophia yet. Noting her friends' confusion, Ellie decided to go first. She channeled the frustration she experienced inside Nicole's brain to levitate Dr. Sophia's candy bowl.

"I assume that is you, Ellie, since Ms. Hurley did not levitate herself," the doctor said wryly. Ellie was taken aback by the comment. First of all, it meant Dr. Sophia knew Olivia didn't have powers. Secondly, it meant Ellie showed no visible signs when she used her power. It surged so strongly inside of her that she never realized no one could see it on the outside.

Kat went next, zipping in and out around the office.

"Brava, Katherine!" praised Dr. Sophia, "That explains the vanishing student rumors."

Nicole stood up from her chair, held out her arms for dramatic effect, and transformed into Dr. Sophia with a wink.

"Ah, so it's been *you* this entire time," surmised the doctor, "I guess that's how you attempted to breech my laptop." Nicole sheepishly transformed back into herself, flushing beet red. Ellie didn't think anything embarrassed Nicole. There's a first time for everything. Chris remained silent. Dr. Sophia nodded at him, then launched into her own story.

"I have the power of empathy," she revealed, in her matter-of-fact manner of speaking, "I can transfer a person's point of view to someone else or reciprocate it, like I did with you two." She explained, gesturing to Ellie and Nicole.

"How did you get your powers?" asked Ellie eagerly.

"From the magic locker. I attended this school," Dr. Sophia explained. Another thought that had never occurred to Ellie. "Experiencing the traumas of others prompted me to pursue the field of psychology. I worked abroad for a while. I felt an inexplicable draw to return here to learn everything I can about the locker and the source of its magic. I found the previous counselor's notes and started from there."

"Have you been to the in-between space?" asked Kat.

"I have traveled the metaphysical plane, if that's what you're referring to," answered the doctor. Ellie had no idea what she was talking about but had more pressing questions first.

"Have you seen Eliza Fritz?" Ellie blurted out, then hesitantly added, "Or the witch?"

Dr. Sophia was clearly caught off-guard by Ellie's questions, but quickly regained her composure. "I have seen things both dark and light in there," she answered with a cautionary tone, "Both will lead you astray. If I have learned anything, it is that every single entity in the universe has many sides. Good and evil are merely an illusion. Whatever you have seen in there, it is not to be believed." The proclamation left a palpable chill in the air. Ellie was afraid to pursue the topic further. She was more torn than ever.

"Ellie has seen Eliza Fritz in the metaphysical plane," Kat told Dr. Sophia, adding, "The in-between space" to her friends.

"How did you know it was her?" asked Dr. Sophia.

Ellie initially thought the answer would be because the girl looked like Eliza Fritz. Remembering what Dr. Sophia said about metaphysical trickery, she formed a more accurate answer: "I just *knew* it was her. I feel a connection to her I can't really explain." She felt stupid saying it, but it was the truth. Ellie expected the doctor to reprimand her, tell her to not trust her gut, to be careful like her friends had told her. Instead, the doctor leaned back in her chair, ruminating on the information.

"When I was a student here, the rumor was that Eliza Fritz went from sheep to wolf practically overnight," Dr. Sophia spoke carefully and deliberately, "Now, this story was passed down over several years;

therefore, we should be cautious as to its accuracy. It was said that the Fritz family were rather odd. The father worked at the old warehouse. He was a real loner. Always unkempt. The mother was reported to only be seen at the grocery store once a week on Mondays, wearing the same red scarf and sunglasses. No one ever saw her face. Rumors were that she was a vampire. People said their house was haunted. Kids would dare each other to ding dong ditch it."

"Where is it?" asked Nicole, clearly excited about the prospect of a haunted house.

"Gone," answered Dr. Sophia, "That part of town was demolished to build the mall. They were mostly old cabins in bad need of repair." The doctor mentioning the warehouse reminded Ellie of one of the thousands of questions in her mind.

"Have you seen a black cat?" she asked. Realizing that her inquiry sounded rather abrupt, she added, "I have seen one in the warehouse but also in the in-between, um, meta place. It seems to want me to follow it."

"I have seen all sorts of creatures, some that should not exist," answered the doctor ominously, "I don't recall seeing a cat, but sometimes I am accompanied by a fox." Ellie amused herself by picturing Dr. Sophia riding a giant red fox through the expanding field they happened upon in the in-between space. "I'm sure you have more questions, but I have an appointment now. I warn you to be cautious, especially with this witch." Dr. Sophia stared directly at Ellie this last part. A rush of calm poured over her, like warm liquid relaxing her brain. Finding Eliza Fritz suddenly didn't feel so urgent. Ellie was thankful for the respite, even if it was only temporary.

As the four left the office, Ellie noticed Olivia in the waiting area. They nodded to each other as Olivia went into her appointment.

"Ha! You knocked *her* into submission!" quipped Nicole. Ellie wanted to tell her friends about Olivia's sister, but she had promised not to. Besides, it was not her story to tell. Ellie decided to change the subject.

"Chris, why didn't you tell Dr. Sophia about your power?" she asked.

"Because she already knew," he answered.

"What? But we promised not to tell anyone!" Ellie exclaimed.

"I didn't tell her it was a super-power, just that I could sense things really, really, really well," he answered, half-embarrassed, half-defensively.

"Did you know she had powers?" asked Nicole, sounding anxious, her face starting to blur out of control.

"No! It's not like that. I needed help. My parents are never around. Now that my brother's gone, I didn't know where else to turn," he looked at Ellie, "I tried to tell you. I just didn't want to be a burden since you have so much going on. But I couldn't eat. I was scared." Ellie's feelings of betrayal melted into concern. She had spent so much energy questioning her friends' loyalty that she hadn't been there for Chris. She wrapped her arms around him. "It's okay," Chris assured her, "Dr. Sophia's sessions have really helped, and Kat's taught me to control it so much better now."

*"Get a room."*

Ellie decided to let the comment slide. She was in a forgiving mood. Perhaps it was an after-effect of Dr. Sophia's power of empathy.

# Chapter 17

# The Fear of Failure

The four ran to Dr. Sophia's office when the dismissal bell rang, only to discover the doctor had already left. As disappointing as it was, the animated chatter of winter break filling the hallways made it impossible to be upset. Ellie headed to the band room to retrieve her trombone. Izzy was leaving just as Ellie got there. Izzy's joyful smile elated Ellie's heart to an entirely new level. It seemed like the Olivia Hurley Incident happened years ago. So much had changed since then. Ellie thought how strange it was that after all the years of abuse she endured, it was Izzy's pain that served as the catalyst for revenge.

After grabbing her trombone, Ellie headed to her locker. She felt a pang of anxiety knowing it would be two weeks before she could try to reach through the back barrier again. The ball of light in the locker seemingly felt the jubilation of the students. It zipped around Ellie's arm as she retrieved her coat. She laughed, playfully trying to catch it. Her smile subsided as her focus turned to the swirling space matter. She instinctively touched her hand to it but hit the back of the locker. No surprises there. She remembered the ball of light she conjured earlier and tried again. Try as she might, Ellie could not grasp onto any one emotion. She attempted to channel her fear of being chased by Tiffany-Ann Trombley, her anger from the constant teasing, the anxiety she had every day while walking to school, but the emotions were fleeting. It was as if she felt...happy. Not just happy: content. There was an unfamiliar complacency inside Ellie.

"Are you staying in town during break?" asked Simon deliciously. Ellie jumped ever so slightly. She hadn't even noticed him approaching.

"Um, yeah. Family stuff, you know?" she answered, trying to shield his view of her locker. Despite her growing confidence at school, she still felt a bit awkward around him. Oh, that wavy black hair! Sigh.

"Me too. Maybe we can meet up for a movie or something. You know, with Chris and the others." Ellie was relieved he added the last part. She didn't think she was ready to marry him in real life just yet. She nodded in agreement.

"Cool, I'll set it up with Chris," he replied. Ellie felt a warm glow in her cheeks as she watched him walk away. She had heard other girls talking about boy's butts. She understood it now. She looked back to her locker and saw a faint pink light emanating from her hand.

"That's new," she said softly, waving her hand around as the light dissipated.

"What's new?" asked Chris, leaning against her locker. Ellie held up her hand to show him the light, but it was gone. "That *is* a beautiful hand," he quipped mockingly.

"Well, it was just pink," she retorted.

"What was pink?" questioned Nicole.

"What, do you all have super-hearing now?" laughed Ellie.

"Not quite," said Kat as she approached the others, "But you were saying something was pink."

"Am I that loud?" Ellie asked, somewhat embarrassed. Her friends' laughter was all the response she needed. She rolled her eyes. "*Anyway*, my hand was just glowing pink."

"That was not on the list of things I thought you were going to say," Nicole said, eyes wide, "Do it again!"

Ellie focused on her hand. Nothing.

"Hmm," commented Kat, "Let's go to the warehouse and see if we can figure it out."

Ellie took one last look at her locker and shut it reluctantly. Nicole grabbed her by the arm and they headed out of school.

When they arrived at the warehouse, Kat turned to them excitedly and exclaimed, "Do you know what this means?"

"Dr. Sophia has powers?" answered Ellie.

"Simon wants to hang out with us?" gushed Chris.

"Chocolate bars are half off at the convenience store?" added Nicole, turning into a convenience store employee.

Kat shook her head in disbelief, "Focus! Dr. Sophia got her powers here. She still has her powers. We keep our powers after graduating!"

Ellie laughed as Nicole jumped around, transforming from person to person, walloping with joy. An uneasy smile spread across Chris' face.

"Tell us about this pink light," asked Kat. Ellie recounted the faint pink light that seemed to cling to her hand. "What happened leading up to it?" Ellie's bright red face revealed the answer. Chris snickered as Nicole transformed into Simon. Kat continued, "Ellie, you told us you channel your power with fear and anger. But earlier the snowflakes were moving when you were happy. Your hand glowed when you saw Simon. I think there's more to your power if you could just figure out how to use different emotions."

Ellie nodded slowly, recalling her dancing mobile. She started humming "Sunshine". One by one, the others joined her. They began to dance around, singing and laughing. The rocks around them began to rise. Ellie allowed herself to truly be in the moment. She pushed aside the anxiety and doubt which always lingered below the surface, and let the joy run through her. She closed her eyes and spread out her arms. She tilted back her head, allowing the sun to warm her face. It was the first time she ever truly let herself experience happiness.

Then she heard the screams. Ellie opened her eyes in alarm to discover she was hovering ten feet in the air. Chris hovered just below her, surrounded by rocks. Kat had one foot on the ground while the rest of her body was suspended in a rift to the in-between space. They all seemed to be stuck, making swimming motions in an attempt to free themselves. Then true panic hit as she heard a low, rumbling growl. Ellie looked down towards the noise. There was a white tiger with shocking blue eyes on the ground, looking up at her. Ellie tilted her head in curiosity as she stared into the tiger's eyes. It was Nicole. Ellie couldn't explain how she knew, she just did. She started laughing.

It dawned on Kat and Chris what was happening. They joined in her laughter and began to slowly and safely float toward the ground. Nicole transformed back into herself.

"I did it!" exclaimed Nicole. "Were you afraid of me?"

"I somehow knew not to be," explained Ellie.

"Dude, tiger thoughts are so weird," said Nicole. Ellie chortled, trying to imagine tiger thoughts. She noticed Kat walking around the rocks with a scrutinizing look on her face. Ellie realized they landed into a sort of pattern. The black cat approached from the dark corner to see for itself.

"Ellie, do you think you could fly us up a bit?" Kat asked. Ellie nodded, taking Kat by the arm. Chris started to sing "Sunshine" again. They all joined in. Ellie pushed away the fear of failure. She and Kat rose steadily up until they could discern the pattern the rocks had formed.

*Help me Ellie*

# Chapter 18

# We All Have Our Vices

"Okay, we have to form some sort of plan," Kat said once they were safely back on the ground. "You!" she shouted at the cat, "Can you take us to Eliza Fritz?" Ellie had never seen a cat roll its eyes but swore this one did before walking back to the dark corner. "I'm a dog person anyway!" Kat yelled. They all snickered at her. It was the first time Kat had lost her cool in front of them.

"Okay, between magic rocks and talking to cats, I'm done for today!" Kat marched off in a huff before disappearing into the meta-whatever. The others were momentarily stunned.

Chris turned to Ellie. "Let's let her cool down. I think she's right on using all of your emotions together. Maybe that's why the witch chose you. Your power could be the key."

"If you say 'embrace your power' I'm going to kill you," she laughed. "Okay, okay, I'll work on using other emotions." Chris nodded and waved his goofy wave. Ellie felt a rush of love towards her friend as she watched him walk away. She inhaled a deep breath and turned her focus to Nicole.

"Dude, is that what it's like in your head all the time?" Nicole asked sympathetically, "You really have a hard time trusting anyone, huh?" Ellie nodded in affirmation. She really didn't know what Nicole may have experienced inside of her head. She felt ashamed. "I'm so sorry. I had no idea what that feels like. I swear I would never do anything to hurt you. I wish there was something I could do."

"You already have," Ellie responded earnestly, "I saw myself in your head. I felt what you feel towards me. I don't know why I ever doubted it. It's just so hard to let people in."

"Years of backstabbing will do that to a person. We all have our vices. I make jokes and steal stuff."

"Speaking of which, do you have any chocolate?"

Nicole pulled a selection of chocolate bars out of her coat pocket with a wink and handed one to Ellie. Ellie didn't know how to approach her next question delicately, so she jumped right into it. "Everything moved so fast in your head! I was completely bewildered, like watching life from a high-speed train."

"Yeah, I get like that a lot," Nicole shrugged. "Sometimes I lose focus entirely. You guys have helped anchor me a bit." Ellie recalled the calming affect her image had in Nicole's brain. It was still difficult to believe anyone could see her that way. She smiled and put an arm around Nicole.

"Whenever the slightest thing goes wrong, I start thinking that everyone hates me again. I feel like that little girl Tiffany-Ann Trombley chased around the playground," Ellie explained.

"You seem so fierce. It's hard to picture you like that." Nicole's words surprised Ellie. What also surprised Ellie was that her arm now looked like that of a child's.

"You're transforming me again!"

"Dude, you were so cute as a kid!" beamed Nicole, pointing at Ellie's face.

Ellie pulled out her phone to see herself. Sure enough, her face appeared just like she did as a child, before slowly transforming back to her current mature self.

"That's incredible!" she exclaimed.

"I don't think it's just me. I think it happens when we connect."

"I wonder if you can do it with anyone?" Ellie pondered the possibilities.

"It just happened. I didn't really think about it. I'll have to try it with the others." Nicole appeared lost in thought. Ellie wondered how fast her mind train was going. She realized how grateful she was for experiencing Nicole's perspective.

"I'm so sorry I got mad at you. It's like all I can see is the locker and how to get through it. It calls to me. I'm trying to heed Dr. Sophia's warning but going in feels like the right thing to do. But I shouldn't have taken it out on you."

"I saw the locker in your mind. I get it, but dude, but I'm worried about you. I don't want you to feel so alone. I guess we all could have done a better job of understanding your urgency in getting to Eliza Fritz. We'll make a move soon. Kat will figure it out. She's the clever one." Ellie stifled a laugh thinking of how the clever one of the group just yelled at a cat.

. . . ● . ● ● . . ●

After dinner, Ellie went to her room to practice harnessing her emotions. She stood in the middle of her room and flexed her arms out like she was about to perform street magic. She chuckled at the thought. After all, hers was real magic. She clenched her hands into fists and conjured up Simon's face in her mind. No glow. She closed her eyes and pictured his backside as he walked away from her earlier. Nothing. She hopped up and down, trying to expel her nervous energy. The rocks' message had unnerved her. There was no denying that Eliza Fritz was trying to reach her now. It was exciting and terrifying. It also renewed Ellie's feeling of helplessness. She considered going into the in-between space by herself, but decided she was not in the right frame of mind. Too many emotions were swirling around inside her head. She tried using those emotions to no avail.

As much as Ellie wanted to keep trying, it was no use. She accepted the temporary defeat. She was overwhelmed, confused, and tired. There would be plenty of time to work on it now that school was out. She put on her headphones and allowed herself to relax.

Ellie drifted off to sleep. She dreamt she was wearing a wedding dress, her father by her side. They were in the mall's food court. Her mother,

Nicole, Chris, and Kat were gathered next to the escalator, all dressed in purple. Simon was slowly revealed as he traveled up the escalator, beaming at Ellie. He looked spectacular in a muted pink tuxedo, light shining brightly from behind him. He disembarked and headed towards Ellie. He took her hand and leaned in for a kiss. Ellie felt a warm glow inside of her. The scene was perfect until she noticed the black cat walking towards her, looking festive in a blue bowtie.

Damn it.

# Chapter 19

# Silvery Star Stuff

"Okay, let's go!" groaned a disappointed Ellie. Her wedding dress dissolved into her usual jeans and t-shirt. A path to the in-between space appeared where the escalator had been. Ellie followed the cat into the meta-whatever-thingamajig.

The path of silvery star stuff gleamed brightly in the distance. Ellie knew she must follow it. The cat led the way with a casual air, ignoring every sight, smell, and sound which tempted Ellie to stray off-path. The most beautiful music she had ever heard echoed down a path made of dreamy, swirling rays of purple light and gold stars. Ellie paused to absorb its beauty. Her head cocked slightly as she saw a cloaked figure materialize at the path's entrance. Elongated pale green fingers emerged from the cloak's sleeves as red eyes glowed from beneath the hood. Ellie barely had the wits to jump back. The path melted away, taking the sublime music with it. She decided to attempt some small talk to keep her mind focused.

"So, what should I call you?" she asked. The cat made no indication that it heard her. "I think I will name you John. No, you don't look like a John at all. Simon? That would be too confusing. Aaron? Tom?

Joseph? Edgar?" The cat stopped. It turned its head and narrowed its eyes. Apparently, Ellie had touched a nerve. It turned back around and continued down the starry path. Ellie wondered why it never occurred to her that it could be a female cat. How sexist of her. "Ok, how about Emma? Claire? Marie?" The cat shook its head in mockery. "You understand everything I'm saying, don't you?" Then a strange thought came to Ellie.

"Are you Eliza Fritz?" she asked. The cat stopped got up on its hind legs, and turned around to face her with its arms crossed. "Okay, no more questions," she muttered under her breath.

Just then, Ellie saw something running from the path to the left, the strong whiff of cinnamon permeating the air as it barreled towards her. At first Ellie could only tell it was a large animal, galloping on all fours. It approached her with unnaturally swift speed. She panicked as the giant red fox headed straight for her. Ellie inhaled the fear into the center of her being. As she exhaled out, a stream of red light shot out of her hand and through the tips of her fingers. She could barely control the surge of power as she lifted the giant animal into the air. Ellie ducked as the fox flew over her, narrowly missing her head. She sighed in relief, only to feel a swift kick on the back of her head. Ellie shook off the dizziness and watched as Dr. Sophia soared down to the ground, trailing after the fox. The doctor turned her head and gave Ellie a thumbs-up. Ellie smiled back at her. *"I am sometimes accompanied by a fox,"* she remembered the doctor saying. Well, that was an understatement.

· · • • • ♦ • • · ·

Ellie spent the weekend hanging out with her parents, something she hadn't done much since making friends. She had texted the others about the saga of Dr. Sophia and the Giant Fox but otherwise ignored her phone. Ellie had forgotten how much she enjoyed cooking with her mother, especially when it came to baking desserts. They made mini apple pies with hearts cut out of the top crust. When the filling started to ooze out of the hearts while baking, Ellie loved them even more. They watched game shows together, at times getting vicious with their competition, all in good fun. Ellie's father even let her pick out the evening board game. He was notoriously picky about what games he would play. There were a few times Ellie almost told them her secret. She had been guarding it for so long she didn't even know how to begin. Instead, she allowed herself to enjoy the time. She missed her friends but was thankful for the mental reprieve. Chris texted her Sunday night informing her that Simon wanted to go to the movies the following day. Goodbye, mental reprieve. Hello, anxiety!

· · · · ● · ● · · · ·

Ellie got up far too early on Monday in anticipation of her not-date to the movies. She waited for her mother to leave for work before sneaking in to try on her make-up. Success was imminent since she had watched some tutorials on the internet that morning. Piece of cake! Except Ellie quickly discovered how difficult it was for her to see what she was doing without her glasses. She leaned over the bathroom sink to get as close to the mirror as she could. She grabbed the foundation and tried to cover her freckles, but they kept popping through when the foundation dried. She applied more layers of foundation and powder. Finally, her skin appeared flawless, but a bit plastic. Blush will fix that. Ellie swirled the brush around in the blush and dabbed it onto her cheekbones. She put on her glasses to inspect her work. One of her cheeks was darker than the other. She removed her glasses and tried to even it out, but one side always ended up darker. She began to get upset as she noticed the foundation was beginning to crack. Yep, she was looking more like an old, sad clown by the second. Just as true panic over her visage set in, Kat and Nicole teleported into her room.

"Oh, honey," gasped Kat sympathetically.

"Dude! What did you do?" laughed Nicole, transforming her face into what was surely an exaggerated version of Ellie's make-up stylings.

"It's not funny!" whined Ellie, secretly appreciating that it was, in fact, hilarious.

"Come on," said Kat, grabbing Ellie by the hand. With a quick rush like being sucked into a vacuum, Ellie found herself standing in what could only be Kat's bedroom. The walls were painted in a soothing terracotta color, in perfect balance with the many plants with leaves of green, yellow, and pink. Two large shelves packed with books and serene statues loomed on either side of her bed. There was an intricately carved table on the opposite side of the room where most teenagers would have a television. On it were meticulously placed candles, bells, and an incense burner. A small fountain stood on the floor next to the table. The room smelled like cedar and zen.

"Here, let's fix this", said Kat gently, as she led them to her bathroom. Ellie stifled a giggle upon entering. It was an absolute disaster zone. Towels, make-up, and hair tools were strewn about everywhere. Ellie tried to assess the number of bottles she saw, but lost count at twenty.

It was utter chaos, and Ellie loved how it stood in stark contrast to everything she knew about Kat.

Kat located the make-up remover...somehow...and went to work. Ellie was more than a bit embarrassed when she saw the copious amount of foundation that was coming off of her clown face.

"You don't even need foundation," Kat practically scolded, "Your skin is flawless!"

"I didn't know how hard it would be to cover my freckles," Ellie lamented, "I hate them!"

"Dude! I love your freckles!" exclaimed Nicole. "Look! I even practiced them on myself!" Nicole sounded so proud, but Ellie couldn't see her without her glasses. Instead, she just smiled.

"Do you want me to show you how to apply a more natural look?" asked Kat kindly. Ellie nodded. Kat showed her what to do on one side of Ellie's face, then Ellie copied it on the other. They applied a small amount of eye shadow, blush, and a neutral lip gloss. Ellie put on her glasses to inspect herself in the mirror. Not bad. She looked to Nicole for approval.

"You look gorgeous, girl!" Nicole gushed. Nicole herself looked ridiculous, face covered in hundreds of unnatural-looking freckles. She saw the clock on the wall. "It's almost noon! Let's go!"

Kat grabbed each of their arms and wooshed them to the movie theatre.

· · · • · • · · ·

The trio manifested in the alley next to the theatre. Ellie wondered what would have happened if someone had been there. As luck would have it, the only thing there was a rat behind a trashcan, eyeing them suspiciously. Nicole stuck her tongue out at it as it slinked away. They walked to the theatre's entrance, where Chris and Simon were waiting for them.

"Are you not freezing without a coat?" Simon asked Ellie. She scrambled to find an explanation why she wasn't wearing a coat through the fog his British accent caused. She had completely forgotten it at her house, having teleported from her house to Kat's during the make-up emergency. At least she was wearing her favorite purple sweater with pink and purple flowers adorning the sleeves. She took a moment to appreciate that she wasn't barefoot.

"I, uh, run hot," she answered, trying to stop shaking from the cold. Bad, bad liar.

They took their seats and chatted awkwardly as they waited for the movie to begin. Nicole and Kat arranged the seating strategically, so Chris and Ellie sat on either side of Simon. The four magic friends had difficulty keeping up a conversation with Simon that wouldn't reveal their powers. Thankfully, it didn't take long for the movie to start.

Ellie could not concentrate on the film. Although she fantasized about him often, she hadn't spent much time with the real Simon. He made her nervous, in both good and bad ways. Normally she would imagine herself and Simon as the characters in the delightful holiday rom com they were watching but doing so caused her more anxiety. She was not ready for this. Ellie braced herself for the inevitable kiss in the finale.

The hapless, afraid-of-commitment male character leaned in slowly to kiss the headstrong, career-driven female.

"Ellie, stop," whispered Nicole. Ellie broke attention from the screen. Simon's face looked alarmed as his popcorn bucket hovered in the air in front of him. Ellie gasped, the bucket fell, and popcorn showered all over Simon.

And...scene!

· · · ●· ● · · ·

The five ran out of the theatre to the alley. Ellie was shaking from both the cold and utter embarrassment, but mostly from the utter embarrassment.

"Here," said Kat as Ellie's coat appeared in her hand through the meta-verse. Ellie put on her coat while Simon stuttered, "What? How? That's amazing!" They all launched into conflicting explanations until Simon said, "I mean, when Chris told me, this is not what I imagined!"

Ellie, Kat, and Nicole all turned to Chris, arms folded, eyes narrowed.

"Oh, come on, I have to hear everyone else's secrets, day in, day out. It felt good to tell my own for once," Chris explained. It made sense to Ellie, but she wished he had asked them first, or at least let them know he had divulged their secret to Simon. Still, Ellie knew she hadn't been a perfect friend either. Kat was visibly upset but said nothing. Nicole nodded in acceptance.

· · · · ●· ● · · ·

As Ellie snuggled into her bed that night, she realized she was not ready for make-up or Simon. The dream world would have to suffice for now.

# Chapter 20

# Auld Lang Syne

New Year's Eve is the most anti-climactic of holidays. You go to a party hoping to find someone to kiss at midnight, make resolutions that last two weeks tops, and hope that the next year will be better. 5-4-3-2-1...the ball drops, fireworks explode, everyone tries to sing "Auld Lang Syne", only to discover no one bothered to learn the lyrics. What an embarrassment. At 12:10 a.m. you realize life is just as dismal as before as you walk home alone, shoes in hand.

Ellie was not quite so jaded on this New Year's Eve. She retrieved snacks and sodas from the kitchen and settled onto the couch with her parents. They reminisced about the past year. Their family tradition was to make a to-do list for the upcoming year, because resolutions never seemed to stick. Ellie's written list was fairly basic considering she couldn't tell her parents her real agenda. They played games until it was time for the ball to drop. 5-4-3-2-1, her parents kissed, cue the fireworks, butcher the song, and then the annual slaughter of "New York, New York" while Ellie and her parents formed a kick line.

Ellie snuggled into bed with a smile. She gazed at her mobile and caused the planets to spin around. Her thoughts returned to the meta-whosit-whatsit. She pulled the notebook with her drawings from their adventures out of her nightstand drawer. It had been a while since she had examined them. She realized the locker only appeared during her solo trips. The key was there somewhere. She scrolled through the photos Nicole took of Dr. Sophia's research. Who were all these other kids? What were their powers? Did any of them hear the witch? Eliza Fritz was missing for decades. Had any of them looked for her? She imagined Eliza somewhere trapped, cold, and alone.

Ellie began to feel the anxiety she had managed to pack away during break. Eliza...the locker. The planets on the mobile spun chaotically. Ellie's focus had always been on Eliza, but the signs were all pointing her to the locker. Ellie knew what she had to do. It was time to resume the search. Inhaling in with renewed purpose, exhaling out her fears, Ellie settled into a slow and steady rhythm, focusing solely on the locker.

She knew a portal had manifested in her room before she even opened her eyes. With one last deep breath, she opened them with resolve. Twinkling lights bordered the trail of star stuff which formed the path. The cat appeared at its entrance with a gust of swirling wind. It seemed annoyed at the disturbance.

"Let's do this!" Ellie instructed. The cat narrowed its eyes, and Ellie felt as though it was examining her soul. It threw her off-guard for a moment. Then the cat...shrugged its shoulders?...and set down the path.

The forking paths held more distractions than ever before. One smelling of cotton candy swirled with pink lights and glitter. Another path formed of lush green foliage leading to a glorious tree full of golden apples. Ellie knew she must resist, although she really did like cotton candy. She saw the locker forming vaguely in front of her. She sighed in relief. There was but one more path to avoid. *"Easy,"* she thought. Beautiful music softly whispered to her. The sublime melody permeated her brain. As she approached the path, she noticed it was lined with little wrapped gifts. Ellie longed to see what was inside of them, but she knew she mustn't. Her feet began to feel heavy, dragging as she tried to pass the path and continue towards her destiny. A creature formed shape as it slowly hobbled towards her. Ellie's feet seemed stuck. As the creature got closer, Ellie realized with horror that its face appeared to be some sort of patchwork-like conglomeration of sewn together skin. It moved haphazardly to balance out the weight of the bag it was carrying. There was something moving inside of the bag, struggling to escape. Without a second to spare, Ellie raised the creature high up into the air and blasted it away with a swift ball of red light. The path fizzled away, and Ellie found she could move her feet again. She took a moment to re-center her mind before starting the final descent towards the locker.

This time the locker manifested more clearly. As nervous as she was, Ellie giggled a little when her locker number G09 danced merrily into position. The other lockers lined up on either side of it but seemed more obscure than Ellie's. Inhale in, exhale out. The locker swung open and sucked her inside of it with a powerful force. Ellie looked around at her surroundings. It looked like she was standing in the middle of space, but it wasn't the galaxy as Ellie knew it. She spotted planet-like orbs glowing in the distance but could identify none of them. Yet it all looked oddly familiar. Then she realized where she was: she was in the world in the back of her locker.

"Help me, Ellie," Eliza's words echoed faintly.

"I'm coming, girl!" Ellie shouted back.

Ellie focused on Eliza's repeating words, "Help me Ellie". She found the figure of Eliza huddled over crying as before, translucent and wavering in and out of shape.

"Help me, Ellie."

"How? Eliza, what do you need me to do?"

"Embrace your power," cackled the witch. Ellie looked around but saw no one else. The cat had abandoned her. Ellie began to wonder if it was a trap. Ellie conjured her ball of light, trying to focus on one emotion at a time. She channeled fear, anger, desperation. Eliza's message continued to repeat in the background. Ellie tried to add happiness to the anger ball but could not grasp onto it. The ball grew larger, alive with hues of reds and blacks.

"Release me, Eleanor," continued the witch, "Embrace your power." Slowly, Ellie started to give in. She tried to remain focused on Eliza's image but faltered. Ellie could feel the witch's hold on her, drawing energy from the ball of angst. "Yes, yes, I can taste it!" moaned the witch. Eliza's words stopped and her figure started to rise. She stared intently at Ellie, a vicious smile spreading slowly across her face. Her head tilted as a demonic laugh emitted from an unworldly smile. The smile split open across her head. Ellie stood in helpless horror as the figure of Eliza Fritz started to shift and twist in a violent rage. Skin melted and bones cracked sickeningly. The form of a woman started to take shape. Bones snapped into position and greyish skin oozed into form. The smell of sulfur permeated the air. As the mouth began to reform, she started talking: first as incoherent babble, then into words, growing stronger as she took full form. "I waited forever. Forever. Stuck. Forever. Finally, you came. You came to my locker. Locker G09. Forever waiting for the light to appear in locker G09." Ellie tried to hold on to what was left of her light. This was wrong. The witch's head snapped towards Ellie defiantly.

"I gave you your power, and I can take it away."

Ellie let go. The ball of light shattered. Ellie fell to the ground. Eliza Fritz stood over her. She was now an adult, but Ellie knew it was Eliza. A long black cape swirled into form across her glowing white body and a tall, pointed hat appeared on her head of long, flowing red hair. She gazed down at Ellie, eyes still shining with starlight. Her gaze was soft at first, but a flash of anger quickly took over.

"Revenge!" shouted Eliza Fritz. The word echoed around Ellie as the wind transported her back through the locker into the school's empty corridor. Ellie stood in shocked silence: alone, confused, and defeated.

# Chapter 21

# The Kindervang

Ellie sat in the hallway sobbing. She could barely wrap her mind around what just happened. How could she have been so foolish? The witch...*Eliza*... was now loose, and it was all her fault.

"This is where I become the villain," Ellie shouted. Her words echoed down the corridor, mocking her. She sobbed harder. She ceased only when she heard footsteps running towards her. Ellie was too downtrodden to be alarmed.

"Ellie!" yelled Dr. Sophia as she turned the corner. Ellie looked up at her, face glistening with tears. Dr. Sophia threw her arms around Ellie. Ellie immediately felt a warm, hopeful sensation envelope her body and seep into her heart. Ellie allowed Dr. Sophia's empathy to wash over her.

"I didn't want to lose my powers. I wanted to help Eliza Fritz. But Eliza was the witch all along! What did I do?" Ellie broke down into tears again. Dr. Sophia picked Ellie up and walked her to her office. Dr. Sophia offered the candy bowl as she sat, but Ellie declined. She did not deserve candy.

"Ellie," began Dr. Sophia gently, "Magic comes from the meta-verse. Students have been given magic since long before Eliza Fritz. That power is yours. It is not hers to take."

"I feel so stupid! I believed everything she said!"

"You're not the first person to be tricked by a witch, Ellie," Dr. Sophia maintained her signature soothing tone. "Now tell me everything that happened."

Ellie recalled her encounters with the witch and Eliza Fritz. Dr. Sophia shuddered when Ellie mentioned the various creatures who tried to lead her astray.

"Kindervang. Child snatchers. Nasty things. Avoid them at all cost," Dr. Sophia warned.

Ellie made a mental note of the word "Kindervang" and continued her story. When she finished, Dr. Sophia took a moment to digest the information. She unlocked her desk drawer and pulled out the folder with all of her research on the Magic Locker. As Dr. Sophia poured through the papers, Ellie found it difficult to keep her hands to herself. There were several items in reach that Nicole had not taken a picture of. Ellie ached to learn their secrets.

"This makes sense," Dr. Sophia said after a prolonged silence. She showed the expulsion letter to Ellie, unaware that Ellie had spent many a night studying it alone in her room. "Eliza Fritz was expelled the day of her disappearance. All of this...the lights, the phenomena...were probably from her locker, which is now your locker. She must have gotten trapped inside. She's been in the metaphysical plane this entire time, waiting for someone to awaken the magic in that locker."

"How did she get trapped?" asked Ellie.

"That's a good question," Dr. Sophia replied. She pulled out an official-looking letter written in the disorganized scribble Ellie had presumed was from the previous counselor. "This states Eliza Fritz was expelled for cruelty to staff and students, but it's oddly vague. There are several records of detentions leading up to it. The earliest ones are for fighting with another girl. The violence between them seems to have escalated over a short period of time."

"The girl was her bully," Ellie stated flatly. "The girl was her bully, and the locker gave her the power to defend herself, but she used it to punish." She knew because it's exactly what she had done.

"That's what I think, too. There's more. Eliza's record indicates there was trouble at home."

"So many of them did," Ellie added, forgetting herself.

"Did they now?" questioned Dr. Sophia with a suspicious but friendly tone. Ellie flushed red as she realized she had just given away that they had gone through the files. Dr. Sophia decided to move on. "Anyway, I think this was all a recipe for disaster. Adding what you just told me to what I read in these accounts, I think Eliza Fritz has some sort of power to create illusions."

"Dr. Sophia, why are you telling me all of this?"

"Because we are a team now, Ellie. We must all be aware of Eliza's capabilities if she decides to strike out. All bearers of magic have a responsibility to protect the non-magic population. Eliza's escape could be catastrophic."

*"Revenge."* Ellie's thoughts fixated on Eliza's last word to her. Revenge on who or what, though? Ellie sat in silent contemplation for longer than she realized.

"Let's get you home. You look exhausted," Dr. Sophia said. "Now, which portal did you go through?"

"What?"

"How did you get into the meta-verse? Which portal?"

"Um, I opened one in my room," Ellie admitted hesitantly.

"Wow, that's very advanced!" Dr. Sophia seemed impressed. As tired as she was, Ellie couldn't help but think of how strange their conversation was. "Well, hopefully it's still open. Let's give it a shot." Dr. Sophia opened the door to her office. Instead of it leading to the school's corridor, it showed an opening to the meta-verse. Ellie gasped.

"How'd you do that?"

"Practice," Dr. Sophia answered. "Now hang on tight," she ordered, taking Ellie by the hand. As soon as they stepped into the portal, the giant fox bounded over them and continued to run. Dr. Sophia jumped into its wind-stream and followed. The chase was like being on a bullet train, or at least what Ellie imagined being on a bullet train would be like. She wondered if Dr. Sophia ever caught the fox. That was a conversation for another time. Ellie noticed with relief that the forking paths were so blurred their temptations were lost to her. She was not mentally ready to face another Kindervang. She wondered if she would ever be again. A pang of shame vibrated through her at what she had done. Dr. Sophia seemed to know how to navigate the in-between space, at least, better than Ellie and her friends did. She let go of the fox's wind-stream at just the right time and they floated gracefully down to the edge of Ellie's room.

"Ellie, please know I am always here for you. I won't let any harm come to you or your friends. Together, we are stronger than Eliza Fritz." Ellie nodded wearily. Dr. Sophia took a step back and vanished, along with the portal.

· · · ● · ● · ● · · ·

Ellie texted her friends to warn them as soon as Dr. Sophia left. All she could do was wait for them to wake up and read the message. She quickly sketched everything that had happened.

Kat teleported into her bedroom with the others in tow sooner than Ellie had expected. She was relieved that at least Kat was an early riser. Chris wasn't as put together as usual. Nicole was still wearing her pajamas and yawning.

Ellie told them what happened. They handled it better than she expected. Ellie was still overly distraught. That can happen when you release a witch from the metaphysical plane. To her surprise, her friends consoled her. Even Kat didn't speak a single reprimanding word. Their support meant the world to Ellie, but she was still going down a guilt spiral.

"So where is she now?" asked Nicole, trying to suppress another yawn.

Chris tilted his head a bit, "I've got nothing. Sounds like a normal day. Maybe that's a good sign."

"She's laying low. That gives us time to form a plan," said Kat, "If you were a vengeful witch who's been stuck in a locker for over thirty years, where would you go?"

"Home" replied Ellie.

"That might be a problem seeing as her house is now a mall, her mother died, and her father is off-grid," said Chris.

"She'll probably start by looking for her father then. That's what I would do," said Kat, "Do we have any leads as to his whereabouts?"

"None. I've tried," replied Ellie.

"Hey, I've gotta go," Chris said a bit too cheerfully.

"Me too. Day with the fam," added Nicole. Ellie couldn't believe they were being nonchalant about a vengeful witch being on the loose. She didn't want to be alone. Ellie looked hopefully at Kat.

"I'll be right back," she assured Ellie. Kat grabbed the others and disappeared. She was back before Ellie had finished brushing her teeth.

"Thanks for coming back. Do you want some cereal?" Ellie asked, stomach growling.

"Sounds good!"

The two settled down and had breakfast. Kat was like the big sister Ellie never had. Her presence had a comforting effect on Ellie, not unlike the warmth of Dr. Sophia's power.

"Kat, can you help me harness other emotions? I can only seem to conjure negative ones on the spot." Ellie wondered if things would be different if she had been able to add happiness to her angst ball. Eliza Fritz seemed to feed off the negative emotions in order to grow the strength to break free.

"Sure, we can try," answered Kat, munching on granola. Ellie turned on the local news to see if anything strange had been reported. It seemed to be an average day. She checked her phone to see if there was anything on social media. There was news, just not the news she was expecting.

"My Sister Cellophane has a new keyboard player!" she shouted with excitement, showing the photo to Kat. "The band welcomes Jem Walker to the band as our new keyboardist," Ellie read aloud "We are excited to share some new music with you soon. Meanwhile, congratulations to our fans who deciphered our clues. The new album is titled "Planets Align". Below is how each clue fits in." Ellie skimmed the clues, "Oh...Henry the VIII...eight planets, I should have guessed that!"

"You are such a nerd!" Kat teased.

After breakfast, they teleported to Kat's room. Ellie remembered to bring her coat this time, just in case. Kat instructed Ellie to sit cross-legged on the floor as she set a little table with a bell, candles, and incense.

"We'll begin with a soothing environment. But remember, you may eventually have to do this under pressure," warned Kat. Ellie nodded her head in resolve. She closed her eyes and allowed the mood to sweep over her. Kat's incense reminded her of some of the pathways in the meta-verse. She heard Kat strike the bell. Ellie instinctively opened her eyes. Kat was sitting cross-legged with her hands on her knees, palms open upwards. Ellie tried to imitate the position.

"Try to get as comfortable as possible. Straighten your back a little more. Relax. You shouldn't feel like you're straining to hold the position," Kat instructed while Ellie fidgeted around, trying to relax. "That's good. Adjust when you need to. Give yourself permission to be calm." Calm. It was practically nonexistent in Ellie's life. "Now think of a time you were happy. Really happy. Take a moment to remember every detail of that moment. What were you wearing? What did you hear? Taste? Smell?" Ellie recalled baking the pies with her mother. She could see her mother smiling. Ellie concentrated hard until she swore she could smell the pies baking: sugar, cinnamon, the browning crust. Birds were singing next to the open window. Yes, she could remember this moment perfectly.

"Open your eyes, Ellie."

Ellie opened her eyes. Warm, yellow light was beaming up out of her palms all the way to the ceiling. Ellie's surprise caused the light to falter.

"Concentrate, Ellie. Keep that happy moment in your thoughts." Ellie did as Kat instructed. The light started beaming unwaveringly.

"Um, so what do I do with it?" she asked.

"I don't know!" laughed Kat. She got up to touch the light. She wiggled her fingers through it. "It's warm! And I feel happy! Ellie, I feel your happiness!"

Ellie laughed along with Kat until a voice crept into her thoughts. *"Embrace Your Power."* Ellie recognized it as her own voice, but it scared her nonetheless. She remembered the horrible image of

Eliza Fritz transforming into the witch. Her light dissolved into nothingness.

"Ellie, what is it?"

"I'm sorry." Ellie started sobbing. "It was just so horrible." Kat put her arm around Ellie and let her cry it out.

"It's okay," Kat consoled, "We're with you." Ellie's gut reaction was to reject the words. As distraught as she was, she allowed herself to accept them.

# Chapter 22

# Ellie's Purple Unicorn

All was dark at the Greenwood Mall. Eliza Fritz stood at its entrance, feeling the bitter cold all the way through her bones down to what was left of her heart. She blasted through the doorway and glided through the splintered wood, dust, and glass scattering in the destruction. Her eyes narrowed as she surveyed the revolting gluttony which surrounded her. She didn't know exactly what she was looking for, but it most certainly wasn't here. Here, where her house once stood. Here, where she toiled away her youth. Here, where her mother kissed her good-bye one last time all those years ago. Her memories now lay in waste under a shiny, new house of disposable fashion, plastic bottles, and fried flesh on a bun.

· · · ● · ● · · ·

Ellie did not know how she was going to function through a normal day as she got ready for school. She couldn't help but worry about what Eliza might be planning. How strong had Eliza grown trapped inside a magical universe? Could she do more than create illusions now? Ellie wondered if Eliza had found her father, if he was even still alive. Maybe she did, they rejoiced, and are currently cuddling on the couch with a hot cup of cocoa, reminiscing about old times. It could happen.

Ellie summoned her trombone and old lady backpack, fixing her curls strategically around her face as the objects slowly floated towards her. With one last look in the mirror, Ellie inhaled in a deep breath and exhaled with resolve to have a great first day back. Her friends were waiting at the front door, chatting with her mother. Ellie shoved a pastry in her mouth, received the obligatory kiss from her mother, and headed out the door. They speculated upon Eliza's next move as they walked to school. It got them nowhere, of course, but it felt better to talk about it.

Chris and Ellie animatedly discussed MSC, Jem Walker, and the new album as they walked to her locker. It popped open for her. The ball of light greeted her. She wasn't sure if it would be happy to see her after the events of New Years' Eve. But there it was, seemingly oblivious to her grave mistake. The swirling cosmos was no longer there, which came as no surprise. Ellie hoped that portal was closed for good. Chris parted, bouncing as he went, waving his goofy wave. Ellie headed to the band room to drop off her trombone. She passed Dr. Sophia's office on the way. There was a sign on the door which read" *DR. SOPHIA IS OUT DUE TO FAMILY ISSUES*". Ellie sighed in disappointment. She felt better when the doctor was nearby. She wondered what could have happened to cause Dr. Sophia to leave at a time like this.

It was a typical day, which made it even more surreal for Ellie. By the time band rolled around, her brain was recovering from chemistry and fractions, which had quickly become two of her least favorite things.

She retrieved her trombone, nodded to Paul, and turned around in her chair to chat with Nicole.

"Ms. Faisal, Ms. McNeil, I see that winter break has made you two even more verbose," Mr. Schwartz' voice boomed across the room. Ellie turned around and straightened up. Nicole became less verbose, depriving them of a witty comeback. "Now, if you will all settle down, we must prepare for the Spring concert!"

Spring concert. It all seemed so normal. Ellie had to suppress a derisive laugh. Come Springtime, she may be performing at the Spring concert or battling a witch to save the universe. Either/or. Perhaps both.

After school, Ellie and her friends headed to Nicole's basement since it was far too cold to be at the warehouse. Even inside, the decrepit walls and broken windows allowed in too much of the winter chill. At least they could have some privacy at Nicole's, but Ellie couldn't levitate too high indoors. She ached to practice, hoping to control it enough one day to be able to fly.

"Dude, stop moping. It's too cold to fly now anyway." Nicole said as she let them into the basement. Ellie didn't realize how obvious it had been. Sometimes she wondered if Nicole could read her mind. *That* would be a daunting power. As Ellie entered the room, she noticed a different snare drum on Nicole's set. She decided not to comment and simply hoped Nicole had returned the school's drum and purchased a different one instead.

Kat buried herself in her phone, searching the news for any unusual events. Nicole took a seat at the drum set and started banging out an aggressive rhythm. Ellie and Chris settled onto the couch.

"If a witch had been seen walking around town, we would have heard about it," Nicole shouted at Kat over her drumming, transforming herself into a green-skinned, wart-covered, cartoon-like version of a witch. Kat nodded her head slightly but kept scrolling.

"Hey, listen to this," Kat said, signaling a disappointed Nicole to stop. "They're saying a car drove through the mall's entrance last night. No sign of the car, nothing was stolen, and the video surveillance was scrambled at the time."

"So?" asked Nicole.

"It was Eliza," Ellie stated solemnly, "She went home." Ellie wondered how Eliza felt, discovering her home was gone. Much had changed since Eliza had disappeared. She must be going through quite a shock. "Revenge". The word once again reverberated through Ellie's brain.

"Dude, she must be so pissed," Nicole quipped.

"Still, no one was hurt. That's good I guess," surmised Kat. "Chris, have you heard anything?"

"No. I've been able to block out noises so I can sleep now," he answered with a shrug. Ellie felt a pang of guilt, thinking once again how grateful she was that she did not struggle with her power like Chris did. "Well, she's on the move, but hasn't caused too much trouble?" He suggested.

"I wonder if she has any idea where her father might be? That is, if he's still alive?" Kat asked. "I assume that's where she would go next, but maybe not. We have to remain alert. 'Revenge' could mean revenge on her bullies. What happens if she looks for them at school?"

They spent the next several weeks on alert, but nothing happened. At least, as far as they knew.

· · · · ● · ● · ● · · ·

Ellie tried to summon a balanced ball of energy for the millionth time. Kat was working with her on channeling her emotions one at a time. Ellie was getting good at that part. Combining them together was the issue.

"C'mon, Ellie, , you've got it this time," Nicole's encouraging words rang out as she retrieved a candy bar from the cabinet.

"Don't distract her," ordered Chris, sitting on the edge of the couch, laser-focused on Ellie's success.

"She's got to work through distractions," Kat replied, "We still have to deal with the Kindervang."

Ellie let out a nervous giggle at the absurdity of their conversation before trying again. *"Anger, fear"* she thought as lights of red and black fused into a ball which floated between her hands. She looked at her friends with determination. She thought of Chris' goofy wave, Kat fixing her clown make-up, and how Nicole saw her when Dr. Sophia swapped their points of view. *"Happiness, hope".* A yellow light streamed out of her hands and wavered around the ball: happiness. Ellie allowed her mind to relax. Deep breath in, slow exhale out, and the light joined the others. Ellie felt something hit her. She looked down at the crumpled piece of paper which had made contact with her head.

"What?" said Nicole innocently, chocolate crumbs falling out of her mouth. "I was just providing a distraction." She transformed into a Kindervang-like creature with chocolate in its mouth. "She has to practice!"

Dr. Sophia had been absent for weeks. Still, they wanted to prepare for when she finally did come back. The reason for her absence was officially "family issues" but Ellie and her friends didn't believe that. So, they practiced and waited.

• • • ● • ● • • •

Eliza Fritz floated through the abandoned warehouse. She wondered how long she had been trapped inside the locker. Everything had changed so much, and yet so little. The life she knew was in shambles, but war, greed, and famine still ravaged the Earth. Yes, the true monsters were here, in this world.

She remembered her father's station had been on the far side of the building next to the windows. As a little girl, she would tap on the window until he gave her a sweet to make her go away. He always had some sort of hard candy tucked in the pocket of his overalls. At least, before everything went wrong.

Her eyes narrowed, honing in on the sudden movement coming from the corner of the warehouse. A black cat emerged amidst a swirl of dead leaves and snow.

"You!" she shrieked. She landed on the floor and ran towards the cat. The cat leapt into the warehouse's portal. Eliza tried to stop herself but went flying through the portal after it.

· · • • · • • · • · ·

Ellie dreamed she was riding a magnificent purple unicorn through the meadow. Her hair was long and golden as it whipped around her head in the wind. She wore a silver crown set with large, oval amethysts. The beast galloped to a halt as they happened upon a curious little cottage nestled between four majestic oak trees. Ellie dismounted the steed, smoothed her shiny purple dress, and adjusted her crown.

The door to the cottage opened as she approached. The welcoming scent of apple pie wafted through the entrance. Ellie let her nose lead the way inside. There was a tiny kitchen to the right. Wooden bowls and spoons hovered all about, mixing wonderous delights all by themselves. There was an assortment of candles on the table. Ellie chose a brass candelabra. When she picked it up, the candles lit automatically. She proceeded towards the back of the cottage. There was a desk with parchment, a quill and ink bottle, and a mirror. Ellie set down the candelabra and picked up the mirror.

"I wouldn't touch that if I were you," rang a voice from behind her. Ellie dropped the mirror and spun around. Eliza Fritz sat in an oversized lounge chair surrounded by cushions, eating grapes. Her feet were propped up on an ottoman revealing black pointy boots with large brass buckles on the sides. Ellie froze in shock.

"Seriously? Blonde hair and a crown? I thought you were better than that," Eliza said nonchalantly as she munched on a grape. The façade faded. Ellie was now dressed in her favorite purple corduroy skirt and sweater with the flowers on it. Her golden hair sprang up into her own brown curls. Ellie brushed them out of her face defiantly.

"Why are you here, Ellie?" demanded Eliza. Ellie did not know the answer. She was just riding her unicorn, minding her own business. Eliza inspected her shrewdly. "I did not summon you. So, what brought you here?"

"A unicorn," answered a bewildered Ellie. Eliza rolled her eyes. Her patience had clearly grown thin. Ellie plucked up some courage and asked, "I want to know what you're planning."

Eliza cackled derisively and waved her hand. The cottage dissolved as the school appeared around them. Students were screaming and running in all directions. Ellie could feel the heat of the fire as it barreled down the hallway toward her. Frantically, she ran to her locker. She tried to open it, but couldn't. Ellie gathered all her strength and held her hand out towards the fire, shooting out whatever emotions she could to combat it.

Ellie woke up screaming. She was in her bed. Her mother burst into the room.

"Ellie! Are you okay?"

"Yeah, Mom. I just had a bad dream," Ellie answered, trying to compose herself. It did not work. She burst into tears as her mother held her.

"It's okay, honey. I'm here," her mother's voice soothed Ellie. She wanted to tell her parents everything but couldn't quite find the words. The conversation would have to wait for another time. For now, Ellie settled for a good cry.

# Chapter 23

# A Secret Portal

Their plan was simple: trap Eliza Fritz back inside the Magic Locker. In order to do that, however, they would need a much more complex plan.

Ellie had the idea to have Chris locate Eliza with his super-hearing, then he and Kat would teleport her back to the school. Chris had been practicing with the blindfold on while Kat teleported further and further. He had been able to track Kat over ten miles away. They really seemed to be gelling into a strong team.

As far as pushing Eliza back into the locker, well, no one knew exactly how that would work. Hansel and Gretel used brute force. They would need something more cunning. Ellie had practiced moving the others with her telekinesis similar to how she did with Olivia's sister. Slowly, she tried adding each emotion. Fear, anger, happiness, hope. Meanwhile, Nicole had an easy time transforming into different animals and had moved on to transforming the others into various versions of themselves. She was usually successful, except for the time she accidentally turned Ellie into a clown. At least, Ellie thought it was accidental. She was still quite embarrassed about her make-up attempt.

"So, Ellie, you think the locker became some sort of metaphysical prison?" asked Kat, retrieving a Kombucha from Nicole's fridge. It would have been impolite not to: Nicole had stolen them just for her.

"Great band name," quipped Nicole, lounging on the couch instead of her usual seat at the drum set, "Metaphysical Prison". Ellie took a moment to appreciate how Nicole's long, blue hair was cascading over the edge of the couch. Ellie was sitting on the adjacent couch, sketching Eliza's cottage with as many details as possible. Kat sat next to Ellie and grabbed the pile of sketches from the meta-verse to review. Again. For the hundredth time.

"Maybe all of us together are strong enough to push her back in," offered Chris, "Like, if we keep our eyes closed, maybe her visions won't affect us?"

"But I felt the heat of the fire," answered Ellie.

"I'm certain Eliza caused the damage at the mall," said Kat, "I think she can manifest visions into reality." They all groaned simultaneously.

"She was in the meta-verse for decades! She could have absorbed its power like some sort of metaphysical sponge," said Nicole, a little too excited at the prospect. Then she snickered, "Metaphysical sponge". Ellie laughed, too. A year ago, she would never have imagined the bizarre conversations they were having.

"We need to stay sharp and move quickly," Kat ordered, "We can't let her torch the school. People will get hurt. We'll have to do it this weekend when nobody's there." The mood in Nicole's basement turned solemn. They all knew Kat was right. The weekend was only two days away. Ellie stiffened her jaw with resolve. They had practiced enough. She was as ready as she'd ever be.

·  ·  ·  ●  ·  ●  ·  ●  ·  ·  ·

Ellie checked Dr. Sophia's office first thing at school the next morning. She didn't expect her to be back; it was more out of habit. Ellie was beginning to worry that Eliza Fritz really had done something bad to Dr. Sophia. Surely that's why the doctor had left, to find Eliza. Ellie shuddered to think of a world without the brilliant and kind Dr. Sophia.

Ellie realized she had been staring absent-mindedly at the sign on the door: *DR. SOPHIA IS OUT DUE TO FAMILY ISSUES*. Something was odd about the sign Ellie had not noticed before. She squinted her eyes. Yes, there it was. The space inside of the "O" was swirling ever so slightly. Ellie touched her finger to the space. Her finger went right through the door. Dr. Sophia had left an open portal.

Ellie ran to her locker. She was thankful to see her friends already there.

"Dr. Sophia left a portal!"

"What?" asked Chris.

"It's in the sign on her door...through the "O"! We can go in and find her!" Ellie was ecstatic. Her friends followed her to Dr. Sophia's door. Kat examined the portal while the others obstructed the view. The portal expanded around Kat as she pushed her arm through.

Kat abandoned her usual caution and turned to Chris. "We can go in tonight after everyone's gone home. Hopefully you can locate her." Chris nodded in agreement. "Okay, everyone! Let's sneak out and meet outside the gym at midnight. Operation Save Dr. Sophia is a go!"

· · · ● · ● · ● · · ·

Ellie was unable to calm the storm inside of her. It was decided that Kat and Chris would go into the portal to look for Dr. Sophia while she and Nicole waited inside the school. Ellie thought it was an unnecessary precaution. They could cover more ground, erm, space, if they all went. Still, she could not deny that something bad could have happened to Dr. Sophia. If the others didn't return in an hour, she and Nicole would go to get help. From whom, exactly, she did not know. But two of them getting lost was better than all four of them getting lost, so Ellie and Nicole waited.

Ellie tried to focus on her breathing while Nicole rapidly morphed into different people. Ellie felt a pang of shame that this behavior ever bothered her. It clearly helped Nicole cope.

"I'm getting snacks from the vending machine," Nicole announced.

"Do you need some money?" asked Ellie.

"Pfft, no!" Nicole answered, turning into the custodian. She held up keys to the vending machine. Ellie managed a nervous laugh to escape through her anxiety as she watched Janitor-Nicole saunter down the hallway, swinging the keys. But Ellie realized that waiting alone was worse. She started to hum "Sunshine". Her voice became louder as she began to sing the words. Her voice traveled through the empty halls and reverberated back to her. The pulsing energy of it felt amazing. As she grew more confident, she started to sing her heart out. The sound of her singing echoed back to her again, but it was joined by another.

"Elllllllllie," the voice sang mockingly.

It was Eliza Fritz.

# Chapter 24

# The Witch's Curse

Ellie froze in her tracks. She looked around for any sign of Nicole. Nothing. Ellie was alone. After a moment of tense silence, Eliza cackled menacingly. Ellie tried to mentally calculate the distance to the locker, wondering if she could trap Eliza on her own.

"Oh, Ellllllllie," Eliza's eerie voice rang throughout the empty corridors. Ellie stood as still as possible. Her heart was beating hard inside her chest. Where was Kat? She and Chris should have been back by now. "Elllllie," Eliza continued, gliding through the halls. Ellie could tell Eliza was close. She decided to make a run for the locker.

She heard Eliza's cackle behind her. A ball of fire launched past Ellie's head. She did not take the time to turn around. She had to make it to the locker. She ran as fast as she could but running was never her strong point. More fireballs flew past her. She allowed the fear and frustration in, and with one long exhale used them to lift herself up off the ground. After a moment of fumbling, Ellie straightened out her body and flew fast around the corner to her locker.

Fire approached from every angle. Ellie crouched down against the locker. She channeled her fear into a protective shield of light. Red flickered all around her. It would not hold for long. Ellie knew what she had to do. Keeping the shield in place best she could, she sat cross-legged on the floor. Breathe in, breathe out. The rhythm was too fast. With a long, concentrated exhale, Ellie closed her eyes, picturing her friends standing beside her. "Fear, anger, happiness, hope," she chanted, summoning the energy of each emotion. She could feel the shield grow stronger. "Fear, anger, happiness, hope," she repeated, holding out her hands to extend the shield further. She began to stand. "Fear, anger, happiness, hope," she was shouting it now with confident defiance. She opened her eyes. Eliza Fritz was surrounded by her own fire.

Kat, Chris and Dr. Sophia teleported next to Ellie. Ellie pushed her mind to enlarge the shield to protect them.

"Where's Nicole?" Chris shouted over the noise of the raging fire. Nicole bounded down the hallway towards them as a tiger. Ellie moved aside. allowing the locker to open. Nicole leapt through the fire and headed for Eliza Fritz. Eliza looked around in panic. Nicole pressed Eliza towards the locker. Ellie held the shield around the others unwaveringly.

"No! No! Please!" begged Eliza as she grasped desperately into the air for something to hold on to as the locker began to suck her inside of it. She aimlessly hurled flames into the air.

"Eliza, you don't have to do this!" announced Dr. Sophia in a soothing voice, "I found your father! He's alive! But he needs help!"

Ellie couldn't quite decipher the look on Eliza's face at this news. Ellie's resolve began to soften. She could see in Eliza the scared little girl who got trapped all those years ago. A girl who suffered abuse from her classmates just like Ellie and her friends had. A girl who deserved a second chance. Ellie extended the shield over Eliza and Nicole. She had to try to save Eliza.

"Ellie, what are you doing?" Kat cried out.

Ellie looked into Nicole's tiger eyes, relaying a silent message. Nicole transformed into human form. Ellie pushed the shield to form a bubble around them. The chaos inside the school suddenly muted.

"Grab hands!" ordered Ellie. They connected hands in a circle around Eliza. Ellie could feel the others' power rush through her. She had an idea. "Nicole, can you make her a freshman again?" Nicole nodded. While Ellie maintained the bubble, Nicole concentrated on Eliza, who was still trying to fight. Slowly, Eliza let go of her anger and morphed into her freshman self. Ellie pressed into Dr. Sophia's power. The air crackled around them, and they felt the fear inside Eliza's mind. Ghostly visions of other students manifested. Eliza cowered as they pushed her, knocking her books to the ground. She bent down to pick them up, and one of the girls shoved her to the floor.

"Eliza Fritz, the cowardly witch!" she taunted as everyone laughed. Eliza quietly tried to gather her belongings. "How's your freak father? I heard he was in quite the bar brawl last night!" the girl continued. Ellie noticed tears swelling in Eliza's eyes. "Aw, at least it wasn't your mom, though, right? My Dad told me he had to visit your house on three domestic disturbance calls last month." Eliza leapt up and punched the girl hard on the face. Ellie could feel Eliza's anger ripple over them like a wave. The far wall burst open and lights as large as planets appeared in the sky outside. It looked like an enormous portal to a place Ellie had not yet seen. Eliza's bully lay helpless on the floor as the other students ran, abandoning her.

"Stay away from me, you freak!" the girl cried out. A large staff manifested in Eliza's hand. She rounded on the girl, raising the staff, ready to strike. The locker swung open and began to suck Eliza inside as she screamed. The malintent Ellie had felt inside Eliza's head paved way to shame and sorrow. Her vengeful anger was gone. Dr. Sophia's power flooded them with a calm, soothing feeling. Ellie grabbed onto Eliza, and fought desperately to hold her back from being trapped inside the locker again, but the force of the vacuum was too strong. It slowly dragged them further in. Just as Ellie couldn't hold on any longer, Dr. Sophia jumped between them and the locker. Ellie and Eliza were knocked to the ground. In a daze, Ellie sighed in relief as she saw the locker slam shut.

With a whoosh, Ellie went back into her own perspective. Eliza wiped away the last of her tears. With a wave of her hand, she repaired the damage done by the fire. She took a long, hard look at Ellie.

"You embraced your power," she said through a half-cocked smile. She shot through the air, forming a portal in the wall. As the portal started to close behind her, the black cat trotted down the hallway towards it. With a tornado-like swirl, it briefly transformed into a man with skin like charcoal and jet-black hair, his eyes glowing unnaturally green He nodded at Ellie and her friends approvingly before transforming back into the cat. He leapt through the portal after Eliza just as it was closing.

Ellie stood up and surveyed her friends' faces. Something was wrong.

"Where's Dr. Sophia?" she questioned in a panic.

"She was sucked in!" exclaimed Chris, pointing to the locker. Ellie opened the locker. The barrier between worlds was gone, as was the ball of light. Ellie touched her hand to the back of the locker. It was solid metal. She turned to her friends. "Nothing's there!" She cried. She punched at it, trying to break through, but the magic was gone. They circled around the locker in stunned silence.

· · · ● · ● ● · · ·

Kat dropped Ellie off outside of her house. They hugged goodbye.

"That was a really kind thing you did," Kat praised as she wiped some ash off Ellie's face. "Are you going to be okay?"

"Yeah, I think so," Ellie answered, forcing the tears from her eyes.

"Dr. Sophia will turn up, Ellie. You said yourself she can navigate the meta-verse really well. She'll find a way out." Ellie nodded weakly.

"Where did you find her?" asked Ellie.

"Chris heard her shouting for help as soon as we went through the portal. We had to focus for awhile before honing in on her location. We teleported in to a forest full of old abandoned cabins. Dr. Sophia was locked inside of one of them. When we let her out, the cabin vanished. We tried to come straight back to the school, but our surroundings kept changing on us. I'm so sorry we took so long."

"It's not your fault. At least that gives us a place to look for her. I'll examine my sketches of the forest for any clues."

Kat nodded then disappeared through a portal. Ellie stood on the front step of her house, feeling completely numb. She wondered if she made the right choice by freeing Eliza Fritz...again. She unlocked the door and went inside. Her parents were up, watching the news on the couch. My Sister Cellophane were on the news.

*Reporter: How long have you had this power?*

*Miles: Since I was thirteen.*

*Reporter: And you said you got this power from your locker at school?*

*Miles: Yes. I knew there were others like me. When we found each other, we formed the band in order to reach other magic users across the globe. We discovered about a hundred so far. Now that we found Jem, we can use his power of amplification to extend our search further and faster than before.*

*Reporter: You have hidden your magic for close to a decade. Why tell the world now?*

*Miles: We wanted other magic users to know they don't have to hide. The source of our magic connects us all. We will find you.*

*We will find you.* The words Miles was repeating in the meta-verse.

"Ellie, you're home! Are you seeing this? Magic is real!" Ellie's mother exclaimed.

"Mom, Dad, I have something to tell you," Ellie said, sitting on the couch between them.

· · • · • · • · ·

And that is how our secret was revealed to the world. No one knows how long the magic locker has existed or how it came to be. There could be thousands or even millions of magic users throughout the world. They could be anyone or anywhere. Be wary of who you tangle with, for the magic locker has a way of testing even the purest of hearts. You never know who has been pushed just a little too far.

Now, if you'll excuse me, I have to go kill my father for murdering my mother.

# Epilogue

Creeping Lily blew through the window and manifested inside of the bedroom. After months of searching for the girl, there she was, asleep in her bed. Creeping Lily stood over the miserable little ingrate with disgust. Her hair flowed over the bed and around the child's neck. But she had to stop herself from ridding her world of this nuisance once and for all. She came here for a singular purpose, and she would have to control her impulses so as not to jeopardize that mission. She would deal with this meddling child and her friends later.

Creeping Lily did what she did best, and crept through the room undetected. She harnessed the wind to expedite the search. The wind blew silently, searching through stacks of school books and journals while Creeping Lily checked the closet. She rifled through jacket pockets, binders, and an old backpack with hideous patches. Modern children had too many possessions. This one was overly fond of purple. How vulgar.

With a desperate sigh of frustration, Creeping Lily motioned for the wind to circulate around the mobile on the ceiling as she stood at the foot of the bed, deep in thought about where the thing she sought could possibly be hidden. Did this child know the significance of it? How could she? Kids these days always had their noses in their phones, oblivious to the worlds around them. Creeping Lily rolled what was left of her eyes. That idiot musician had revealed the truth about magic to the world, and nothing would stop her from taking full advantage. All she had to do was find what she was looking for before someone else did.

The wind searched under the bed. Moments later, a journal flew out onto the floor. The wind swept through it, revealing its contents. Creeping Lily saw drawings of various Kindervang, an old hut, the Changing Forest, a purple unicorn...seriously, why are the unicorns always purple? Don't these kids have any imagination?...ah, there it was! Creeping Lily spread out her decaying fingers and snatched the drawing of the Disappearing Cabin.

With one last contemptible sneer, Creeping Lily disappeared with the wind.

Moments later, a portal appeared in the room. Hafeez jumped out, remaining in cat form while he surveyed his surroundings. Papers, notebooks, clothing, and knick-knacks were strewn about the floor. Creeping Lily had already been there. Panicking, he checked on the child. With a sigh of relief, he saw that she was safe. Transforming back to his original form, he used his magic to put all of her belongings back in their rightful place.

With one last look at the room through his piercing green eyes, he jumped back through the portal, relieved that the human, Eleanor McNeil, was safe for now.

# About the Author

Elara Dunn lives in Marietta, Georgia with her husband and twin daughters. She is an accomplished fiber artist, specializing in weaving.

While participating in GISHWHES, Dunn realized the magnitude of the long-term effects bullying had on herself and others, shaping her into a fierce ally for those who deal with emotional and physical abuse. The idea of writing a book series centered around bullied kids came to her in a fever dream.

Dunn has always been interested in how other people live and has studied different cultures and religions. Understanding and embracing both our differences and commonalities has been a driving force in her life. She is a passionate civil rights advocate and volunteers assisting others with disabilities.

In her spare time, Dunn enjoys board games, trivia, and cosplay. She is an avid watcher of Jeopardy! and Wheel of Fortune. She hopes one day to own a red Plymouth Fury and order one of everything at the diner.